meet again. – Rod Gilley, Founder & CEO of RDG BOOKS PRESS

CW01500547

# Acknowledgments

I would like to say a big thank you to my wife Gemma and daughter Lilah-Poppy for their ongoing support.

You both make me laugh every day!

To Mum, who encouraged a love of fiction by buying me the books of Roald Dahl when I was a young boy, and Dad for fuelling my love of cinema. No-one had a VHS collection as large as his when I was growing up, and from a young age, watching the films of Hammer Horror and Alfred Hitchcock no doubt had an influence on my developing tastes.

May you both continue to rest in peace.

I would also like to say thanks to Rod Gilley and the team at RDG BOOKS PRESS for helping me bring this creepy little tale to life.

Mark T. Bates

# MARK T. BATES

# The Curse of Six

*Kierh*
*All The Best*
*Mark*

First edition

Editing by Rod Gilley
Cover art by Lia's Publishing

This book was professionally typeset on Reedsy.
Find out more at reedsy.com

*"For Lilah-Poppy & Teddy ..."*

# Contents

*Foreword*                                    ii

*Acknowledgments*                             iv

Part 1 Chapter 1                               1

Chapter 2                                      3

Chapter 3                                      7

Chapter 4                                     12

Chapter 5                                     18

Chapter 6                                     23

Part 2 Chapter 1.                            28

Chapter. 2                                    31

Chapter. 3                                    36

Chapter 4.                                    41

Chapter 5.                                    45

Chapter 6.                                    53

Part 3 Chapter 1.                            62

Chapter 2.                                    72

Chapter 3.                                    77

Chapter 4.                                    86

Chapter 5.                                    90

Chapter 6.                                    93

*About the Author*                           98

*Also by Mark T. Bates*                     100

# Foreword

"Mark T. Bates delivers a Gripping, Powerful tale." – Rod Gilley

The author worked tirelessly to bring you this story, hoping so much to entertain you.

Please consider leaving a review on
  https://www.goodreads.com/
  and
  https://www.amazon.com/

Reviews are Life's Blood for Authors.

RDG BOOKS PRESS is proud to present "The Curse of Six", the first novella we ever published. Mr. Bates has a bright future ahead. Be looking for his next book, 'A Slow Decay of Flowers' 2026 via Baynam Books Press, and many more to come!

Haven't heard of RDG BOOKS PRESS? Check out our website here: https://rdgbookspress.com/

Love the cover of this book? Check out the artist's website here: https://liaspublishingservices.wordpress.com/

Thank you for joining us in "The Curse of Six", hope we will

# Part 1 Chapter 1

The wind and rain battered my face as I peered over the edge of the cliff. It was dark, but not so dark that I couldn't see down the sheer drop to the raging waves as they crashed violently against the rocks some 500 feet below.

I contemplated my mortality in the seconds before I am driven towards my suicide, for they say your life flashes before your eyes in the moments before you die. And if that was true, then I wasn't going to enjoy the visions that accompanied my final breath as I plunged towards the deep.

I stepped back a few paces and nervously looked around for my tormentor to see how close she was, before glancing to the moon for comfort one last time. And as I breathe in one large gulp of air to provide me with the courage to leap to my fate, I could almost taste the darkness.

I had come close to death's cold embrace a number of times before, but jumping in this moment, from the highest point on the cliffs of Beachy Head on the English south-coast, was inevitably going to be the final time this morbid pull plagued my existence. For I faced a certain fatal drop onto a bed of jagged rocks, before being pulled into a particularly rough current that would take my lifeless body out to sea.

The Grey Witch, who had previously tried but failed to summon me to my death on numerous occasions, would finally fulfill her desire to claim my soul for herself. The horrible apparition would be the last thing I saw before I succumbed to oblivion; her ghostly image I once again had the displeasure of gazing upon through the haze of the torrential down-pour. A demonic vision in a dirty grey veil who was surely smiling underneath, as she knew that I was finally hers.

# Chapter 2

The first time I brushed close with death was twelve years earlier; I was just six years old. A near-tragic accident, as far as my mother was concerned, but one that was orchestrated by the hand of the Grey Witch.

My memory of the whole ordeal had always been pretty hazy. I was certainly too young to really know what I was doing when I sunk down under my bath water and held my breath until I passed out. My father was gone, and I would never see him again, that much I did know. He was killed instantly when he lost control of his car, slamming the vehicle into a wall as he drove home from work a couple of weeks earlier, on the evening of my birthday.

I had been waiting for him to return with all the excitement and apprehension a small child has on that most special of days. I wondered what gifts he may bring home for me.

As I grew older, I learned a little more about his death. That his neck had been broken in two, snapped from the impact as if it had been nothing but a wishbone. His face and torso had been ripped to shreds by the contorting metal and shattered glass of his car. It was a closed casket at his funeral. It was on the day of his funeral that I was almost drowned.

I never saw my mother cry once in the aftermath of his death. Looking back, I would go as far to say that she almost seemed relieved it was just going to be me and her from that moment on.

At his funeral was a lady, dressed head to toe in a grey shoal at the back of the church. This was the first time I had seen her; a mysterious figure who kept to herself, and who no-one else seemed to acknowledge. She was a constant presence during the service, a presence who seemed to be watching me through the murkiness of her veil. I found that I was repeatedly drawn to this curious figure and regularly checked over my shoulder as the vicar said his words beside my father's coffin.

I didn't know who she was, or why she kept her distance from the rest of the congregation. She was blurred by her veil, and I couldn't see her face, but I remember clearly that she was incredibly tall. On one occasion that I had glanced over my shoulder, I am sure that her arm had raised, and her finger pointed towards me, as if she wanted to be sure I knew she was there. Eventually she no longer was.

Later that evening, it was just myself and my mother left at home following the somber wake she had held in our house. My mother ran me a warm bath before bed as she always did, before leaving me alone to play.

I lay there thinking about my father and tried once again to understand the loss. The fallout following his death had been like a whirlwind for me, and in that moment, for the first time I truly realized the finality of death.

His funeral had made everything feel complete, but I yearned to speak with him one last time. It felt as if I wasn't given the chance to say goodbye. As the shadow of a figure flashed across the bathroom wall, for the first time in my life, I felt a feeling of pure and utter despair.

In a trance-like state, I wondered if I sunk down under the bath water for long enough to fall asleep, that I might somehow arrive at a place closer to where my father was. I wondered whether I might be able to see him just one last time and ask him why my mother didn't miss him. I remember closing my eyes as I let my body drift down into the water, and I visualized my father's face.

After a minute or so, I was coming to my limits of breathlessness, and the need to resurface and take a gulp of air took over my senses. I opened my eyes and prepared to lift my head out of the water. But as I looked up, I saw *her*, watching me through her grey veil, seemingly hovering just above the surface of the bath water. I watched helplessly as her arm outstretched, and her hand pushed down onto my chest. She pinned me down to the bottom of the bath; I was too small and weak to put up much of a struggle. And there I remained, as the mirage of her veiled face turned to darkness.

Time passed, I cannot recall how long. The next thing I knew I was awaking to an awful commotion; my mother pushing hard on my chest and blowing air into my lungs. I was naked and laying on our cold bathroom floor, bruised and grazed from where she had dragged me from the bath in a desperate panic. For the first time that day my mother was crying. Her tears turned to the uncontrollable sobbing of relief when my eyes opened, and I coughed. She held me in her arms, and for what felt like an eternity, we lay there together. She wouldn't let me go.

"I can't lose you. I can't lose you," she repeated endlessly, before finally pulling away and looking into my eyes. "What happened, Stevie?"

And in that moment, I honestly couldn't recall.

# Chapter 3

D espite the unquestionably caring nature of my mother, who tried to do her very best for me as a single parent, the loss of my father had ultimately led to many unhappy childhood years that I largely spent in a haze of loneliness.

Even in primary school, I found making close friends a difficult task, often preferring to spend time in my own company rather than playing with other children. I sought comfort and solace in books, taking after my father I believe, as some of my strongest early memories were of him reading to me at bedtime. From an early age I had immersed myself in the dark fairy-like tales of Roald Dahl and had begun exploring our local library and the classic novels harbored within its walls. This was my therapy.

Growing up towards the end of the twentieth century, there was little information on juvenile mental health, and little support for single parents with awkward shy children. My mother and I never spoke of what had happened to me the evening of my father's funeral. Any memory I had of the mysterious woman dressed in grey had seemingly vanished from my developing mind. The years passed by rather uneventfully, and ten years later, I was finishing my final year at secondary school, a boy of sixteen with an uncertain path ahead of him.

Like my father, I was fairly tall for my age, and I had a mop of thick jet-black hair just like he did. In rare moments when my mother let her guard down, she would look at me as if studying my face, and tell me I reminded her of him, when they had first met. I thought about my father and remembered his face every day; from the stubble around his lips, to the childhood scar that sat high on his left cheek.

I cherished a number of photos of him that my mother kept in a box, and I longed to learn more about him and his past. I knew he was born over in Ireland in the sixties. Then he moved over to England and was adopted as a small boy after he was orphaned. From what I was told, he was passed from one foster family to another while he grew up.

There was one Polaroid of him with his birth mother in the box of photos we had. It was the only picture of her he had owned. My mother told me he had only ever remembered her name as *Mumma.* There was no record of his father. Written in pencil on the back of this particular photo was a year; *1973* ... and they both looked incredibly happy.

\* \* \*

As my eleventh school year drew to a close and my GCSE exams loomed heavily, something rather unexpected happened to me. I met a friend, and she would leave an almost inconceivable impression on my life. Polly Robertson joined our school after the Easter holidays purely to sit her final exams. Her parents had moved down to our small coastal village in somewhat of a rush from Edinburgh, after her father had been offered a job opportunity too good to turn down.

I was smitten with Polly from the first day that she sat down next to me in our English Literature class. I remember looking up as this beautiful blonde-haired girl with freckles across her cheeks was brought into the classroom by the deputy head-teacher. Polly had walked across the class towards me and smiled as she sat down.

"This is my first day and I'm a little nervous," she whispered.

I think I was just as nervous as she was when I awkwardly smiled back at her and shrugged my shoulders.

At the time, I was writing a study of the themes within Bram Stoker's *Dracula*; a piece of work which, as it turned out, would get me a solid A grade. Polly pulled out her notepad, pencil case, and a copy of *The Turn of the Screw* ... and I knew we were going to be friends.

At the end of the lesson, when the coast was clear to talk, I plucked up the courage to properly introduce myself. And we ended up sitting on the field in the early Spring sunshine, eating our lunch together.

I like to remember how inseparable we were during the following weeks. We enjoyed the same alternative rock music, and of course we had a love of the same classic gothic-horror books. She genuinely seemed to enjoy spending time with me. It was as if she was a gift sent from heaven to pull me out of my shell and into the real world.

Polly and her family had moved just two streets away from where I lived with mum, and we soon started walking to school together in the mornings. We would often study together in the evenings. My mother seemed to absolutely adore Polly, almost as much as I did. I think seeing me socialize and grow close to someone warmed her heart. She would tease me when we were alone and tell me how lovely it was to see me with my '*Girlfriend*'. But I hadn't actually thought of Polly as a girlfriend, after all, as close as we had become in such a short space of time, we hadn't spoken about whether anything more was happening between us. We just hung out as friends, and it felt right.

"Are you going to ask Polly out on a date?" my mother asked me one morning during breakfast, causing me to spit my mouthful of Cornflakes out in alarm. "You need to let her know how you feel, Stevie. She is a lovely girl, and someone like her is not going to stay single for very long."

I excused myself from the table and gave my mum a look that rubber-stamped how awkward I found the conversation. But as I left the room, I thought to myself that she was probably right. Polly had been living down here for a couple of months at this point, and she already had more friends in school than I did. I couldn't let her slip through my fingers, and was fairly sure she felt the same way as I did.

So that evening while I was sitting on my bed and she lay on the floor engrossed in her schoolwork, I decided to make a move. But instead of asking if I could take her out on a date as I had initially planned, and should have done, I did something incredibly stupid.

I slowly slid down from the bed and lay beside her, and as she rolled onto her side to face me, I put my hands on her hips and kissed her firmly on the lips.

"Stephen!" Polly shouted sharply as she pulled herself away and quickly scrambled to her feet. "What on earth are you doing?"

I remember the instant feeling of dread as the words left her lips, and the realization of just how wrong I had got this hit me hard. "I'm so sorry, I just wanted to give you a kiss. I thought you'd like me to?"

"No. I have no idea why you'd think that. I thought we were just studying together. I thought we were friends."

"I'm so sorry," I repeated, bewildered at her reaction and the impossible situation I now found myself in. "I just thought, you know. That it was maybe about time we, well you know?"

"No, I don't know. This is really fucking weird. I think I'd better leave now."

And with that, she scooped up her stuff and was out of my room before I had the chance to say another word. I sat on my bed and waited for the sound of the front door shutting. Then I started to cry.

Within a few minutes, I heard my mother coming up the stairs.

"Stevie," she called out as she reached the top. "Was that Polly leaving? She never said goodbye." Mum arrived at my door and saw the sorry sight in front of her. "Darling, what's wrong?"

I told her what had happened, and she walked over to the bed and sat down.

"I'm sure everything will be okay," she tried to reassure me. "You just need to speak with Polly tomorrow and tell her how you feel. Explain that you didn't mean to offend her." She thought for a moment, before finishing her advice, "Maybe you should have told her you had feelings for her before you tried to kiss her though, Stevie."

With that, my mother kissed my head and said good night. I was left alone. I sent Polly a simple text message before I went to sleep that night.

*I'm sorry x.*

She didn't reply.

# Chapter 4

The next day, Polly didn't show up at school. It was a Friday, and that evening I text her again.

*I'm really sorry Polly. Can we meet up tomorrow and talk?*

This was met with further silence. In fact, I didn't hear from her all evening or the following day. As time went on, a feeling of uncontrollable anxiety started to take over me. I had really messed up. I felt like I had lost the only close friend I had ever made. I also began to worry that when I went back to school on Monday, everybody was going to know what I'd done, and I'd be a laughingstock. I began to sink into a deep depression.

Mum kept telling me everything would be okay and that Polly probably just wanted a few days of space, that she'd soon forgive me as we'd been such close friends. But deep down I knew nothing would be the same with her again. I clearly remember the overwhelming feeling of dread that I felt about even going back to school and facing her after the weekend. A deep, familiar feeling of loneliness I had felt for years before she came into my life began to overwhelm me.

I had no real close friends during my teenage years, and I couldn't believe I had done something so stupid as to ruin what

I'd found with Polly. She had meant the world to me.

My mood sunk lower and lower, till on Sunday morning, I could barely bring myself to leave my bed. I feigned illness so that my mother would leave me be, and each time she came in to check on me, to bring me water or some food, I had wiped away the tears to try and hide the pain I was feeling.

That afternoon my mother had planned to go out for a few hours to meet a friend, and she convinced to me to come downstairs and see her off. I stood on the porch and watched her reverse down the driveway, and as she pulled away, I looked across the street.

There, to my surprise, standing in the rain, was a vision that immediately shook me to my core. It was the mysterious lady dressed in grey from the night of my father's funeral, the same dirty veil covering her face. She seemed to be staring straight at me. I shuddered, as the recollection of a distant yet oddly familiar memory sent a cold feeling running down my spine.

As my mother's car disappeared out of view, the Grey Lady raised her arm and pointed right at me, just as she had done in the church those many years ago. I closed my eyes and shook my head, trying to rid my mind of the combined feelings of anxiety and fear. *Who was she?* Eventually I opened my eyes and was relieved to see she was gone. *Had I imagined her?*

I walked back inside our house and shut the door. My heart was thumping so hard in my chest that I could hear it against the silence. I slumped backwards against the door and looked into our living room.

In a split second, it felt like my heart stopped beating altogether. There she was, standing just a few meters in front of me. She was close enough that I could see her yellow eyes piercing through her veil, dancing like fire. I could smell her dank, moldy looking clothes, and I saw her veil move as she turned her mouth up into a smile. I now felt sure that she was some kind of witch, and I watched helplessly as she once again raised her arm and stretched out her finger.

"*Siiix ...*" she hissed at me.

"Leave me alone!" I screamed back at her; slamming shut the living room door that provided a barrier between us. My adrenaline started pumping and I bolted upstairs as fast as I could. For some reason, as if not fully in control of my own senses, I headed straight to the medicine cabinet in my mother's bathroom.

It was full of pills, *Codeine*, *Vicodin*, all manner of different sleeping aids. I frantically gathered the numerous small pots in my arms and ran out onto the landing, where I froze. The Grey Witch was now stood at the bottom of the stairs, her arm still pointing up towards me. Her finger bent and twisted, with the nail a sharp point, circling the air like the head of a striking Cobra.

"*Siiiix ...*" she screamed at me this time.

Her body started slowly moving up the stairs, but she wasn't moving as if she were taking each step one by one, no, she was floating towards me.

"Fuck off!" I shouted, before turning and running into my bedroom.

Shutting the door behind me as quickly as I could, I dropped one of the small bottles onto the floor. I pulled across the latch, locking the door, hoping this was now a border of safety behind me. *But will it keep her out?*

Not knowing what to do, I made straight for my bed, placing my head under the pillow to try and block out any sound of her.

There was silence for a moment. But then it started. A slow

yet ominous knocking on the door. *One. Two. Three. Four. Five. Six.*

I lay there shivering with fright and waited until the knocking stopped. I removed my head from under the pillow which was now damp with a combination of sweat and tears, expecting to see the Witch standing before me. But there was no one there.

My mind was swimming and consumed with fear brought on by the appearance of this phantom who had returned to me. *But why?* I felt like my brain was going to implode.

The pain I was feeling was joined by the thought of Polly, and what I had done to destroy our friendship. I started sinking lower. I was breathing heavy with my heart thumping violently in my chest, and I looked down at the bottles of pills scattered across my duvet.

I fumbled with the top of the closest one, the label said *Temazepam.* I did not know what they were or what that meant, and I did not care. The cap came off and I poured the entire contents into my mouth. The pills were small, and I washed them down with a drink of the water that sat on my bedside table. Then I grabbed the next bottle, the same pills. I repeated, opening bottles and swallowing pills until all the bottles were empty. When I was finally finished, I lay back and closed my eyes.

Memories of Polly, distorted with images of the vile Grey Witch, flashed through my mind. I knew in that moment, that I wanted to die, to escape from all of this. I began to drift off into what I believed would be an endless slumber.

\* \* \*

My desired eternal peace was interrupted when my mother

came into my room to check on me. I was drifting in and out of consciousness, with vomit splattered across my chest and dripping from my chin, the empty bottles of her medication scattered around my bedroom floor.

"Stevie!" I heard her shout as she pulled me up towards her, just as she had done when I was six years old. She then called an ambulance, and by all accounts had caught me just in time.

I was taken to hospital where my stomach was pumped clean.

* * *

In the days after, as I lay recovering at home while feeling incredibly sorry for myself, I once again began to forget about the terrifying apparition I had encountered. Images of the demonic looking Grey Witch, who had returned to me for the first time since the day of my father's funeral, soon dissolved into the ether of my mind once more.

She had appeared when I was at my lowest point, seemingly tipping me over the edge of my sanity, and I had come close to losing my life once again.

I had said nothing of her to my mother, and soon I forgot. The whole affair a suppressed memory my subconscious did not want to believe was real. A little over a week later, I was back at school, and I started the process of sitting my exams, normality seemingly resumed.

I excelled in English, History and Music, and although I saw Polly again in class, she decided to blank me during those final weeks of term, avoiding me wherever possible. This also felt the same with pretty much everyone else at school, as the news of my rejected move on Polly and subsequent visit to hospital had spread like wildfire. Even the teachers would scarcely make eye contact with me. It felt like I had no support outside of my home. Problematic teenage mental health, a taboo subject in the education system it seemed.

That summer, I completely drifted apart from Polly, or should I say she drifted herself away from me. But I would never forget the friendship we had shared, however brief it had been.

# Chapter 5

These two memories had hit me like a flash. The recollection was vivid and arrived in precise detail; yet it felt like I had only just leapt from the cliff edge milliseconds before. These were the first two times I had met the Grey Witch, and I know now that she would come again, and again.

She always appeared when I was at my most vulnerable, when I was weak, and she felt the right to claim my soul for herself. The gap between my first two encounters with the demonic entity had been ten years, but sadly her next visit would not take so long.

Two years after I had finished high school and a few months after I turned eighteen, I found myself living in London, studying English literature history at university.

The rejection I had received from Polly when I was sixteen had knocked my confidence beyond belief. I once again had very little social life during the following couple of years I was at college. I preferred to spend my free time at home listening to music, watching movies, and of course reading.

My mother seemed happy to have me around, pleased for me to be within arms-length where she could always keep an eye on me. We never mentioned the night she found me near comatose, but she certainly never kept prescription drugs in her bathroom again, or anywhere else I might stumble across them for that matter.

As I grew into manhood, it was clear that she wanted me to spread my wings and start living more of an independent life. It had been her who had strongly encouraged me to continue my studying and attend university. My thinking was that I either did this or would have to start working, and I had no idea what I wanted to do with my life.

My father had a life insurance policy which apparently would more than cover the fees for me to study and live in London for the necessary three years.

Within a few weeks of moving into the halls of residence, I became terribly home sick. I'd never spent so long away from the security of my childhood house and the mother who had single-handedly raised me from the age of six. To say I had taken myself out of my comfort zone would have been an understatement of huge proportions.

I shared a room with a pleasant enough Scottish lad named Marcus. The irony of his nationality was not lost on me, and of course reminded me of Polly. He had moved down to the city from Glasgow, and we were somewhat thrown together, victims of circumstance. Two young strangers each living away from home for the first time.

However, despite Marcus having traveled far further from his parents than I had from my mother, he seemed over the moon to be living in London, away from his family. He was there to fully embrace and relish the opportunity of his newfound freedom, and our experiences of university life were looking to be quite different from day one.

Over the first couple of weekends, Marcus went out on the town with a group from his Media class, while I stayed in our dorm room, studying, reading, watching TV, or tinkering around on the acoustic guitar I had taken with me. I soon felt lonely and isolated in a place that did not feel like home.

By the third weekend, I was seriously questioning whether this was going to work for me, or whether it would be best to admit an early defeat and head back to my mother with my tail between my legs. I was seriously considering the prospect of closing the door on my education and facing a reality of having to find employment. But I had no idea what that might look like.

I equally had no idea why I was at university studying English literature history in the first place. *Where was it going to take me once the three years were finished?* I genuinely had no clue. My anxiety was through the roof at this point, and I could feel myself sinking into the all too familiar state of depression that plagued my life.

On the third Friday night that I was living in London, Marcus could see I needed cheering up and insisted that I join him on a trip to the pub that evening.

"Steve mate, you've got to come out and have a few drinks," he told me. "It's not doing you any good staying in all the time. You've only left the room to go to your lectures and that's not what university life is all about mate. Come and have a couple of beers and meet the guys from my class. What's the worst that could happen?"

I had protested a little. But on this occasion, I let him twist my arm. After all, I felt he was probably right, *and what did I have to lose?* Marcus grabbed a couple of bottles of beer out of the fridge and handed one to me.

"Here, one to get us started."

We sank the drinks before heading out into the evening, my first night on London town. We walked ten minutes into Covent Garden, and I found myself in a pub called *The Nags Head*, where a group of Marcus's friends were already occupying a large corner table in the bay of a window. As soon as they saw us, a couple of lads stood up and beckoned us to their table.

"Marcus, Marcus over here mate," a tall fellow with blonde hair and a crisp white England rugby shirt shouted. "Who's your friend?"

"This is Steve."

His friend nodded in my direction. "Nice to meet you Steve, I'm Leo. Take a seat you two, I'll pour you a drink."

There were half a dozen of Marcus's friends at the table, all male, all terribly loud and brash. In the middle of the table were a number of large four-pint jugs of frothy lager, and a collection of glasses. Leo poured drinks for me and Marcus, pushing them along the table in our direction. "Down the hatch boys!"

And that is how the next few hours went by. Drink after drink with loud boisterous, and often obnoxious chatting between the group of friends. All whilst chain-smoking Benson & Hedges cigarettes. I don't think I bought a drink or even got up from my seat in that time, except to maybe use the loo. Each pint poured for me would be accompanied with a slap on my back and some kind of shot, *Tequila, Sambuca, Rum.* These guys didn't let up for a minute.

As the drinks kept coming, I could slowly feel myself slipping into an anxious shell. I just couldn't do anything to stop it. Marcus was enjoying himself and was completely lost in conversation with two of his friends across the table. I was seated next to Leo at the other end of the table. He had his back to me, while he chatted and guffawed to whoever was on the other side of him. I couldn't even tell you the rest of their names. I sat there in silence, just watching, as everyone else enjoyed themselves. I might as well have not been there.

Eventually, I started to feel very drunk. This night out was the first time I had ever drank spirits. Sure, I'd enjoyed a beer or two on occasions before, and for the last year or so, mum had made sure there were a few bottles in the fridge for me. But the drinking these guys were doing was on a whole other level, and I was struggling to keep up. Sitting there in silence for maybe ten or fifteen minutes, completely invisible to the rabble around me, I started to feel incredibly queasy.

I stood up, and stumbled into the corner of the table, knocking over a glass about a quarter full of beer. Leo turned around sharply.

"Woah there fella," he laughed. "And the first spill of the night goes to our new friend Stuart!"

With this, he whacked me hard on my back, and everyone stopped talking, turning to look at us.

"My name's Steve," I slurred back at him, while my eyes felt like they were crossing, and Leo's head divided itself into two floating variations in front of me.

"Are you alright Steve?" Marcus asked.

"I'm fine, don't worry," I replied. "I'm just going to use the little-boys room." And with this, I staggered off towards the bathroom. Within seconds, everyone at the table had turned back to their previous conversations and I was once again forgotten.

# Chapter 6

When I was sure I was out of eye shot of my new *friends*, I changed direction and walked out into the cool autumn evening. I decided to take myself back to the halls of residence, imagining that I would throw up in the bathroom, before passing out face first onto my bed. But as soon as I had started walking, I stopped and froze.

There, across the street, watching my every step, was the Grey Witch. She stood motionless, facing me, but not close enough that I could see through her veil. In an instant, my memories of this phantom-like creature flashed through my mind. Images of her at my father's funeral, and that night through the ripples of my bath water; vivid memories, as if these happened just a night ago. I could feel the weight of her hands pushing down, holding me under in the tub.

I then remembered her haunting me in my own home years later, as I tried to find sanctuary in my bedroom. Before popping one pill after another.

The Grey Witch raised her arm and pointed one long crooked finger across the road at me. I turned away and started walking as fast as I could, the chilly air on my face combined with my fear seemingly helping to counteract the effects of the alcohol

I had consumed. After a time, I looked back over my shoulder, and she was there, maybe ten yards behind me. Floating toward me. I ran, not looking back again. I have no idea how I managed to stay on my feet in my intoxicated state, but after five minutes or so I had reached my halls of residence. I fumbled at the lock of the communal door, but managed to let myself in. Quickly closing the door behind me, I leapt up the stairs to the first floor before fumbling nervously again at the lock. I then quickly entered mine and Marcus's shared room, before slamming the door shut behind me.

I stood inside with my heart beating in my chest, while sweat poured from my brow. My intoxicated vision deceived me. Staring through a foggy haze, I watched the room swimming from side to side, as if caught on the precipice of a wave. Remembering how drunk I was, I stumbled to our kitchenette to pour myself a glass of water.

I downed my drink in one gulp. I was breathing heavy, my body not quite knowing how to react with the level of alcohol in my blood stream, and the intense run I had just put it through. Not to mention the fear of once more seeing the Grey Witch, a vision that I now remembered all too deeply. And she terrified me.

Next to the kitchen sink in our dorm was a window that looked out onto the street. I slowly pulled back the curtain, fearful at what I might see, hoping there would be nothing there. But through the rain, I saw her standing on the pavement across the road. She was looking right back at me.

A feeling of pure dread came over me as I stared at the entity and watched as she once again raised her arm and extended her finger upwards. Her arm appeared to somehow rise from her body, pointing towards me, but now also moving up towards my window as if she were reaching for me. Slowly but surely the crooked serpent-like finger of this creature rose through the air, getting closer and closer until her wretched bony hand was right in front of the glass. I could clearly see her probing nail, which was long and dirty with what looked like dried blood encased within the cuticle. It was razor sharp like the talon of a bird of prey, and it slowly began tapping on the window. *One. Two. Three. Four. Five. Six.*

Then it stopped, and with her poisonous looking nail resting on the glass, she wrote three letters in the sitting mist ... *S.I.X.*

I hadn't exhaled since first seeing the Grey Witch on the street below, and I breathed out a lung full of air onto the window. I let the curtain drop back down, before stumbling backwards. Tripping over our coffee table sent me tumbling over, and I knocked my head hard on the floor, before everything turned black.

\* \* \*

Sometime later in the darkness, I felt a pressure on my throat which caused me to awaken and start coughing. Something was constricting below my chin. I was seated on the floor at the far end of our room, my back to our bathroom door. There was a ligature around my neck, fastened tightly around my throat. I fumbled at the constricting material which felt like leather, and realized it was my belt – the other end was tied to the door handle.

The weight of my body was pulling on the ligature, making the coarse material coil tighter and tighter around my throat. I tried to raise myself up by my legs, but I could barely move, while my arms hung heavy and numb.

Looking up, I saw the Grey Witch on all fours on the ceiling, squatting like a spider ready to pounce on her trapped fly. Her head twisted abnormally from the ceiling facing down towards me, and her piercing yellow eyes glowed through her muddy veil. She started to cackle, a hideous noise that I will never forget.

"*Cursed you are to die, and your soul will be mine. Just like your fathers,*" she croaked menacingly.

She darted across the ceiling on all fours, moving at an unnatural speed towards the window, which was open with the curtain blowing inwards from the wind. As I watched, I felt my eyes roll backwards, and the room turned to black once more.

In the darkness, my mind was swimming with thoughts of the specter that had seemingly attached my neck to the bathroom door via my own leather belt. *And what was it she had said about my father?* Life was draining away from me as the belt constricted tighter, and I gave up the fight. My life was hers, whoever she was.

And just as my thoughts dissipated into an infinite nothing, I experienced a strange sensation of falling, my face crashing to the floor, before someone shouted my name, repeatedly.

Opening my eyes, I found that I was indeed laying with the side of my head on the floor, a pair of trainers standing in front of me. With all the strength I could muster, I looked up. Marcus was there before me, a serrated kitchen knife in his hand, and a look of sheer panic across his face.

"Steve your awake! Thank Christ your awake. What have you gone and fucking done mate?"

I reasoned that Marcus had cut the belt free from the door handle, and it dawned on me the scene he had walked in on. My eyes darted towards the ceiling and then the open window. There was no sign of the Grey Witch.

26

I attempted to tell Marcus that I hadn't tried to hang myself, that it was her. But my throat was raw and dry, no words would come out.

"For fucks sake, Steve. I'm going to call you an ambulance." Marcus sat down on the floor beside me and took out his phone, shaking his head as he dialed. "You didn't need to do this mate. You really didn't. What if I hadn't of come back to look for you?"

I tried to speak once more and managed to splutter the words, "Grey Witch ..." But he couldn't understand me.

"I'll get you some water mate," Marcus said as he pulled himself up, tears running from his eyes. "Yes, ambulance please," he spoke into his phone. And as he walked towards our kitchen sink, I vomited and passed out again.

# Part 2 Chapter 1.

*What is happening to me?*

\* \* \*

I found myself once again admitted to hospital. This time I had been taken there in a state of complete unconsciousness, and I am told I had been in a coma for 48 hours. A result of the ligature around my neck bringing me to the brink of death, as it starved my brain of the oxygen it needed. This time, after I had woken up and was no longer required to be confined within the walls of the intensive care unit, I was not allowed to be discharged. I was not permitted to go home. Instead, I was transferred to the psychiatric wing of the hospital where it was explained to me that I would remain in order to be monitored for at least a couple of days. I was Incarcerated under the Mental Health Act for assessment until my release was signed off by a senior practitioner, and it was deemed I no longer remained a danger to myself, or anyone else. I was still weak and in no position to protest. The following day, I was told I would have a consultation with my assigned doctor.

I was also advised that my mother would be visiting. She had already been to the intensive care unit while I had lay sleeping and had spent a number of hours holding my hand. She had already been called, told that I was now awake, and that I was being transferred to somewhere more comfortable.

I knew how relieved she would be at the news and would be wanting to see me again as soon as she was able to. I wanted to see her too, to let her know that I was ok. But I was also incredibly nervous of what she would think. To her, this would appear to have been my second suicide attempt in two years.

I appeared to all who knew me, to be a sick and troubled young man. *But it wasn't me – I didn't want to hurt myself.* They transferred me by wheelchair through the hospital, down many sterile corridors, a seemingly infinite labyrinth of white walls, and then, via a lift, to a separate wing of the building. I was taken to a room with a single bed, a bedside table, and a solitary armchair in the corner. Encouraged to rest that night, and after being given a bottle of water, a bowl of tomato soup, and a slice of toast, I was provided with some medication that immediately made me feel drowsy.

As I was drifting off, I looked over to the door which had a large window in the upper middle section. And the last thing I saw before falling asleep, was the face of a blonde female looking in at me. *Polly!?*

\* \* \*

On my first night in the psychiatric ward, my dreams were disturbingly haunted. Flash images of the strangers I had met in the pub, all sitting around the table and laughing at me, as I swung by my neck from the rafters over the bar. They were pointing, mocking me – even Marcus – my existence worthless to them. The Grey Witch's voice served as background music to their taunts, '*Cursed you are to die, and your soul will be mine. Just like your father's.*'

I dreamed of Polly. I had become a stranger to her, and in my sleeping vision she was with Marcus. They laughed and pointed at me as they fornicated.

I could feel sweat dripping from my body, seeping into the bed sheets, as I tossed and turned. '*Just like your father's.*'

I felt a hand clasping my arm pulling me downwards. It felt like I was falling, being dragged from the bed. Looking down, not knowing if I was still dreaming or awake, I shuddered as piercing yellow eyes stared up at me. A long snake-like arm rose up and grabbed me, and sharp fingernails began digging into the flesh of my bicep. Hearing the unmistakable cackle of the Grey Witch, as she began pulling me down towards her, I screamed at the top of my lungs, pulling back with all my strength, as my eyes opened in sheer terror.

Then, a flash of light as two nurses came running into my room, flicking the light switch on as they came rushing to my bedside in a state of panic.

"Stephen! Calm yourself down. You're having a nightmare," one of the nurses shouted as she grabbed hold of me to stop my tumbling to the floor, then pulling me back up onto the bed. "You're soaked through, you poor thing." She turned to her male colleague and shouted, "Give him a shot, quickly!"

Before I knew what was happening, I was being held down and there was a large needle in my arm.

I blacked out, and this time I did not dream at all.

# Chapter. 2

I awoke to a room full of people.

"Ah, good morning to you Stephen," the closest of them said to me. "I'm Dr. West and I'll be looking after you until, well, until you get back on your feet and we can send you home. How are you feeling today?"

I looked around the room at the strange faces all watching me and waiting for me to answer and took a moment to adjust myself to having been woken up. "I'm feeling OK," I eventually replied softly, as my eyes then darted to the side of my bed and I shifted my body over to look underneath. There was no-one there. I looked back to the doctor and asked, "How long do I need to stay here?"

"Well, that's totally up to you, Stephen. We need to watch you for a little while, bring you back up to speed. Your mind and your body have gone through quite the trauma, I'm afraid. And you seem, well, jittery to say the least." The eyes of the doctor looked to where I had just checked with a concerned look on my face. "What do you think is under your bed?" I looked at him not quite knowing what to say in reply. The doctor eventually broke the awkward silence for us both. "Never mind, Steven. I can assure you there are no monsters down there. We're going to undertake some therapy to try and help you understand why you did, what you did. We'll help you get to the bottom of everything, don't you worry too much now. You have some breakfast and then shower, get dressed and stretch your legs." He placed his hand on my shoulder. "We have a common room with a television as well as some board games. You can meet some of our other guests there today. Don't be shy, introduce yourself. Now I believe your mother …" the doctor checked his notes, "ah yes, your mother is visiting you after lunch, and then we'll have our first session. Just you and me. We can talk through everything then." And with that he turned around and walked out of the room, his entourage following closely behind.

I did as Dr. West had instructed, and after a cup of tea and some toast, I showered in the small bathroom attached to my room before venturing outside.

I tentatively looked around the corridor. A young woman walked past as I stood just outside of my doorway, and I instantly recognized her as the nurse who had come to my room during the night. She stopped and turned to me, wearing a comforting smile as she did so.

"Well, good morning to you, Stephen. My name's Dawn, we met briefly last night, you may not remember though. I hope you ended up sleeping well in the end. Are you looking for the common room?" I nodded in reply, and she pointed down the corridor. "It's at the end of the hallway there. There are a few people up and about, sitting in there already. You go and make yourself at home. I'll come and see you in a little while with some medication."

I nodded and smiled back at her as I made my way down the corridor. I thought about the meeting I would be having with Dr. West. My first priority must be to get myself out of here as quickly as possible. I knew I wasn't crazy, that I hadn't tried to kill myself. The memory of my encounter with the Grey Witch, the ghostly presence who had appeared once again when I was at my lowest, was still firmly in my mind. But if I told the staff in the hospital about her, they would never believe me, especially Dr. West who, in my brief encounter, had worried me. It would be the perfect reason for him to justify keeping me here in this hospital.

*'Your soul will be mine. Just like your father's.'* These words she spoke continuously rang in my mind. What the hell did she mean? I felt I needed to talk to my mother, to find out if she had any idea what this all meant. Did she know who the apparition was? And what did she have to do with my father? My mother was the only person that gave a damn about me, the only person I could trust--maybe, the only person who could give me some answers.

My head was swimming as I entered the common room and looked around; a large television sat in the corner just as the doctor had said. The longest wall opposite the entrance had a row of windows the entire length across, and there were a number of chairs and sofas dotted around, as well as a few tables with newspapers and magazines on top.

There was maybe a dozen or so people in the room, some sat in isolation looking up at the television. A few groups of two or three sat around the various tables. One group was playing cards; another was playing Chess. A few people looked up at me for a moment as I stood in the doorway, but then soon went back to whatever they were doing.

In the corner of the room, sat a girl with long blonde hair. She was the girl I had seen looking into my bedroom the evening before. At that time, as the drugs were taking over my senses, I had thought she was Polly. But now I could see that she wasn't, although she still seemed strangely familiar. She was staring straight at me, and it made me feel a little uncomfortable, so I quickly broke my unintentional eye contact. I peered around the room once more and made my way over to an armchair, keeping my distance from the girl who I could still sense was watching me, and sat myself down next to one of the windows.

I looked out over the grounds of the hospital, across a vast green space of beautifully landscaped gardens. The view made me feel a little more relaxed, and I guessed that was the idea. After a while of watching the serene outside space, I looked around the room again. To my surprise, the blonde girl was walking toward me. She sat down on the nearest chair, smiled, and joined me in looking out the window.

"It's a lovely view isn't it," she said with a soft Irish accent. "I've spent hours looking out of these windows, watching the birds in the trees. There are squirrels too."

"Oh," I replied, "I'm sure there are." We sat in silence for a short while before I asked her, "How long have you been here?" A question she ignored.

"I like looking out best of all when it's raining. You don't see as many animals, but it looks so pretty when it rains." She turned and looked into my eyes. "I'm Yasmin, it's nice to meet you." She then looked away quickly, and as her eyes seemed to watch the sky she spoke again. "We need to talk somewhere a little more private Stephen."

I was taken aback. "Sorry, excuse me, what did you say? How do you know my name?"

"It doesn't matter, please don't worry." Yasmin looked around the room a little nervously, "You just have to listen to me. You're in trouble, aren't you? I can see your aura Stephen, and there is something, well, someone attached to you. Watching you. She's always watching you."

As these words left her lips, I stood up sharply and paced around between her and the window. "Look, I don't know who you are or what you think you know, but this is crazy."

"Well of course its crazy Stevie, that's why we're all in here isn't it?"

*Stevie? Did she just call me Stevie? Only my parents had ever called me Stevie.*

"You must listen to me. You have to believe me. I have a gift, and I can see certain things. Things you can only imagine." She turned her eyes to the window. "You see the small circle of trees in the far corner of the garden there? They let us outside after lunch. Please meet me there at 3pm. I'll try and explain to you what I felt, what I saw, when you walked into the room." And with that Yasmin stood up.

She looked into my eyes again and smiled. Then she walked away and left the room. I was left standing by the window confused and somewhat scared to say the least.

Given our situation, it occurred to me that Yasmin may well be somewhat unhinged. But what she had said strangely rung true, and I had no idea how she could have known my name, let alone the trouble I was in. I knew instantly that I would be meeting her again to find out what else she had to say for herself. I was drawn to her for reasons I did not know.

# Chapter. 3

The next few hours passed as I sat by the window, exchanging only the odd smile, or nod of the head, with the rest of my fellow patients gathered in the communal lounge. I read some magazines, but my mind wandered, constantly lost in thoughts of ghosts, witches and evil spirits. Trying to work out how I was going to confess what was happening to me when I spoke with my mother. *'Just like your father's ...'*

I was trying to plot my exit from the hospital, but my thoughts continuously returned to the brief encounter with my new friend.

At some point, Nurse Dawn visited to provide me with some more medication. I didn't even ask what it was. She left me with a lunch of egg sandwiches, fruit and lemonade.

A short while later she returned to collect my empty plate. "I hope your food was okay, Stephen. Your mother's here to see you now. If you come with me, I'll take you to the visitation room. You can go for a walk through grounds after if you like. It's lovely and warm out for this time of year."

"Thank you." I replied.

I followed her out of the common room, and we walked a short while, past my bedroom and through a number of hallways, before eventually arriving at a blue door with 'visiting lounge' written on it.

Dawn turned and looked at me with her comforting smile once again, "Your mum's through there, I'll see you later."

I smiled back as Dawn walked away, then I tentatively turned the door handle. Inside, there indeed was my mother sitting on a sofa alone in the room. She looked anxious, and when she saw me peering at her, she burst into tears.

It had only been a few weeks since I had last seen her (I unfortunately had no recollection of her sitting with me while I lay comatose just a couple of days before.), but she looked older than I remembered, and older than her forty something years. Her hair was beginning to grey, and she had noticeably lost weight. Probably due to the stress I had caused her.

I walked across the room and sat down beside her, taking her hand as I did so. She embraced me, holding me tight, just like she had the evening of my father's funeral on our wet bathroom floor. Eventually, she pulled away, her eyes had dried, and she finally spoke.

"Stevie, I've been so worried about you. What have you done to yourself? Why?"

I took a deep breath, struggling to find the right words. "I'm okay Mum, really, I am. I just need to get out of this place and come back home with you. I promise I didn't do what you think I did."

"They told me you tried to hang yourself. Your roommate found you barely alive. He caught you just in time and called an ambulance just like I had to do two years ago." She started sobbing again. "Please tell me what's wrong? What can I do to help you?"

We sat in silence for a while, both of us crying, before I finally plucked up the courage to ask her what I really needed to know.

"Mum, what really happened to Dad?" Why do you never talk about him?"

She thought for a moment, taking her time to reply to my question which had seemed to take her by surprise. "It's been too painful to talk about him and what happened."

"I know mum, but you never cried for him. It feels like you wanted us to forget about him almost as soon as he left us." She looked down at the floor as I continued, "Do you remember what happened to me the night of his funeral? I remember clearly now."

"Of course I remember, Stevie. You almost drowned."

"You saved me. Just like you did two years ago when I swallowed your pills." I gripped her hand tighter. "But both times, I wasn't alone."

She looked up at me. "What do you mean you weren't alone?"

"There was someone with me mum, and she wanted me to die. A woman ... a Witch. And she's come back to me again."

My mother stood up and started shaking her head as she walked across the room. "Stevie, what you're saying is making you sound crazy."

"Mum," I interrupted sharply, "She's trying to kill me, and I think she's got something to do with Dad."

My mother spun around and looked at me with distress in her eyes. "This is ridiculous. You're not well, you don't know what you're saying." I gazed up at her, wanting compassion, a semblance of understanding, anything. "Stevie, I've spoken with Dr. West and told him I want you to come home with me as soon as possible. He is one of the best psychiatrists in London and he has a partner close to us at home that he can refer you to. You're going to be seeing him this afternoon. Listen very carefully to everything he has to say and please don't mention anything like this to him. I want you to come home where I can look after you." She sat back down beside me and this time she took my hand. "I've spoken to your university, and you can start over next term, after Christmas. We need to get you better before you go back." She hugged me tight, looked into my eyes and then kissed my forehead. "I'm going to go now, but I'm hoping I'll be back to pick you up in the next day or two. I love you Stevie, please don't you ever forget that."

And before I could say anything to stop her, she stood up and walked out of the room. I did not follow. I sat rooted to the spot, frustrated that I hadn't been able explain myself well enough to her. Frustrated that she had not listened to me like I had imagined she would.

A few minutes later Dawn walked in. "Stephen, I hope everything's OK? I know how worried your mum was and how desperate she was to see you. Let me take you outside so you can get some fresh air." I followed Dawn as we left the room and took a lift down to the ground floor. From here we walked out into the sprawling gardens of the hospital. "Take a walk, relax and enjoy the Autumn sun while it lasts. Just make sure you stay on the grounds as you haven't been granted permission by Dr. West to leave just yet. And we wouldn't want to have to report you missing to the Police."

I nodded so that she knew I understood. "What time is it?" I asked.

"It's just coming up to 3 p.m. Don't forget you're seeing Dr. West at five, then afterwards, I'll see you again at dinner."

She gently touched my shoulder before leaving me as I looked around the garden, and for just a moment, I found myself

39

enjoying the warmth of the sunshine on my face.

# Chapter 4.

I could see the garden was enclosed to our particular wing of the hospital; an extension added to a rather grand Victorian building. Large walls surrounded the space I had been allowed to explore, with gates seemingly locked to keep us in. If one was so inclined, it would probably not be impossible to scale the wall and make a bid for freedom. But I had a feeling the medication they supplied us with kept the patients docile enough to keep any attempts at escaping the ward to a minimum. I was confident that I would be able to talk my way out of here soon enough, after all I wasn't insane, and I knew that I wasn't a danger to myself. The only danger I faced was the Grey Witch. But after trying to explain this to my mother, it had confirmed for me that I would be foolish to mention her to Dr. West. I would simply tell him what he wanted to hear and was sure I would soon be released into my mother's care.

I began making my way down to the far corner of the garden, to the circle of small trees that Yasmin had pointed out earlier from the window, when she asked me to meet her. I wasn't sure why, but I looked around to make sure I wasn't being watched by Dawn or any of the other nurses. I felt as if meeting with Yasmin was somehow illicit. I couldn't see her as I made my way down, but as I approached the clearing, which was well-hidden from the ground floor windows of the hospital, I eventually saw that she was sitting under the farthest tree.

She was humming softly to herself and making a daisy chain. At the sound of the crackling undergrowth beneath my feet, Yasmin looked up, twisting and turning the daisies in her fingers as she did so.

"Stevie, you came! Here, come sit with me." She invitingly patted the ground next to her, and I walked over, not really knowing what to say or what I was expecting her to say to me. "Thank you for coming to meet me," she spoke through a warming smile, and then looked away as she fiddled once more with the daisies in her hand. "Do you know that some people consider these to be a weed? I think they're beautiful. Just look at that amazing natural yellow colour." She played with the daisies in her hands a little longer, twisting their stems around, and then looked back up at me. "I've asked you to come down here so I can try and help you, Stevie. Will you let me help you?"

"How do you know my name, and how do you know I need help?" I asked, positioning myself next to her and sitting cross legged on the ground like a school child.

"Everyone in here needs help, but I'm especially worried about you, Stevie." She surprised me by taking my hand in hers. "Can I read your palm?"

"You want to read my palm?"

"Yes, if you don't mind? It might help me see what's been happening to you – what's going to happen to you. You see, I come from a long family line of palm readers, and sitting down here within the shadow of the trees is the perfect place for me to connect with you." She looked deep into my eyes. "The aura that surrounds you terrified me when you first walked into the lounge. True there is a darkness that surrounds everyone in our little corner of this hospital, but there's something different about you Stevie. You carry a mark."

I was really struggling to comprehend what Yasmin was saying to me. Talking about auras and reading palms, it made little sense. Yet I could see a sincerity in her eyes, and I knew that I was being haunted by the Grey Witch. If Yasmin could provide me with some answers, then who was I to deny her? I turned my hand over, so the palm was facing her.

"Both please." she smiled, taking my other hand in hers. "Every woman in my family has been able to read palms going back generation after generation," she explained, while intently studying the lines on my hands, her eyes darting across my palms as they followed the patterns. The comforting smile soon disappeared from her face. "I'm afraid to tell you what you already fear, but I believe your soul is marked, and has been attached to a vengeful spirit." She looked up at me. "You've seen her haven't you Stevie? She's the reason you're here, isn't she?"

I was in a state of shock as I listened to what Yasmin was telling me. "How could you possibly know what I've been going through?"

"I know it's difficult but believe me. I told you I have a gift. It's kind of why I'm in here. I can sense the spirits around us, and I can see the past and sometimes the future in the palms of the living." She looked back down at my hands. "Your future however is not so clear. I can't see through the darkness." I could say nothing in reply as tears began to swell in my eyes. I sat quietly, as a wind began gently blowing through the leaves of the trees around us, some beginning to fall to the ground. "This probably sounds incredibly strange to you Stevie, but trust me, there will be a way for you to break this curse, for want of a better word, that you've been afflicted with. There is always a way. As curses can be cast, they can be broken. You need to keep fighting and look into your past for answers." She started shaking my hands in hers. "Get well and take yourself home, away from this place. Find the reason this is happening to you Stevie, for only when you truly understand who it is that wants to harm you, will you be able to break free."

*Just like your father's ...*

# Chapter 5.

Yasmin and I sat quietly together in the clearing for a short while, it was calming, and I am not sure if I had dozed off under the influence of the medication. For when I checked my watch, it was coming up to 5 p.m., and I realized I had been with her for nearly two hours. I had my meeting with Dr. West coming up and I needed to go. I said goodbye and left Yasmin, who said she wanted to stay and read a while, and made my way back up to the hospital. As I stepped inside the conservatory from the garden, I found that Dawn was waiting for me.

"Oh, there you are Stephen. We were worried you'd fallen asleep somewhere and were about to send out a search party. Come with me to Dr. West's office, he's ready to see you now."

I followed the nurse down the hallway until she eventually stopped at a door, with '*Dr. M. West*' engraved on a brass plaque, and knocked three times.

"Come in," the doctor called out from the other side of the door.

Dawn turned the handle and peered inside the room. "Good afternoon doctor, I have Stephen McCarthy here for you."

"Thank you, Dawn. Send him in."

She turned and beckoned me into the room. Dr. West was seated behind a large mahogany desk. He stood up and walked around to greet me.

He was a tall man, maybe six one or six two. He was wearing a brown tweed jacket with what looked like an expensive fountain pen tucked into the top pocket. He was an imposing figure who exerted confidence through his very demeanor. I guessed he was aged around fifty, he was slightly graying in his immaculately combed hair.

"Stephen." He extended out his arm and grabbed my hand, shaking it firmly. "Or do you prefer Steve?"

"Steve is fine," I replied.

He showed me to a red leather chair on the opposite side of his desk, and I sat down. He walked around and sat back down himself. Looking at his computer screen, he began tapping on his keyboard for a short while, then he picked up a ring binder from his desk and started flicking through, humming as he did so. My name was on the front of the file. Eventually, the doctor looked back at me and put the file down on his desk.

"So, Steve. As you know I'm head of psychiatry here at the Nightingale Hospital. This is your second day with us, following your spell in our intensive care department. The doctors looking after you there felt you'd benefit from a period of respite in here with us before you go home. And well, to be frank, how long you spend with us is going to be up to you, and the discussions we have here in this room. Do you understand everything I've said so far?"

"Yes, I do." I nodded.

"It's my job to determine from speaking with you whether or not I feel you pose any further danger to yourself outside of these walls. You are currently under a temporary Section, which means we can keep you lawfully detained. But believe me when I say, we want you to go home, Steve. I don't want to keep you here a minute longer than necessary. Sadly, beds are at a premium on our ward, and we always have people waiting to come in and see us. I need to decide whether your recovery is best spent here, or at home with your mother."

"Thank you," I replied. "I want you to know that what happened the other night, well that just wasn't me. What I mean is, that I was not in my right frame of mind. I had no prior intention to harm myself, and I have no intention to do so in the future. I'm afraid I can barely remember what happened. You see, I blacked out from drinking too much alcohol. I'd been drinking heavily all evening, and it's the first time I've ever done so to that extent. It changed me, and I don't want to ever drink that much again, it was horrible."

The whole time I was talking, Dr. West watched me carefully, taking in every word as he did so. When I finished talking, he plucked the fountain pen from his pocket, turned a couple of pages into the folder on his desk, and wrote some notes.

"You say this was the first time you'd drank alcohol, Steve?"

"To that extent yes. I'd been out with my roommate and his friends, and we'd been drinking a cocktail of different shots. I think there was vodka, rum, whiskey ... I've only really ever drank beer before, no more than a couple in one evening. And well, I'm ashamed to say, but the last thing I remember clearly was being sick in the pub toilet. I then came back to my dorm, and well, I really have no clear recollection of how I got there."

Dr. West continued scribbling into his notebook before looking back up at me. "This is an interesting perspective on the evening, Steve. The records do indeed confirm extremely high levels of alcohol in your blood." He hummed to himself again and tapped his pen a number of times on his desk. "They also tell me you've been in hospital before, a couple of years ago. This is a pattern of behavior forming that we certainly need to be helping you with." He looked straight at me, his eyes meeting mine without blinking. "Steve, tell me about your father?"

I have to admit I hadn't expected the sudden change in subject, least of all for him to ask me this. Nobody ever spoke to me about my father. "What do you want to know? I'm not sure I understand?"

Dr. West nodded in reply. "Well, you see Steve, I had a consultation with your mother this morning. Before you saw her. I wanted to know about any past trauma you had faced in your life, to understand if she felt there was anything that had made you do, what you did. She explained to me that you lost your father when you were young." He paused for a moment. "That must have been very hard for you?"

I thought for a while before answering, staring out of the window behind his desk. "Yes, I suppose it was. He died in a car accident when I was six. In fact, it was on my birthday. I missed him terribly, but Mum, well she didn't seem to. We never really talked about him while I was growing up."

"Losing a parent at that age has a great psychological impact on a child. If you and your mother never spoke about him, then you will have had many suppressed feelings waiting to come out. You see, I feel this is the root to the feelings of despair you may now be experiencing as a young adult. Were you thinking about your father when you tied your belt around your neck Steve?"

His bluntness was a surprise. "I can't remember, everything was a blur. As I told you, I blacked out." As much as I wanted to, I couldn't tell him about the Witch, I couldn't tell him what really happened. He never would have believed me. "I believe

I was thinking about him before I went out that evening. I was wishing he had watched me grow up, and that he was here to see me at university. I was sure he would have been proud."

"Yes Steve, I understand." With this the doctor continued writing and we both sat in silence for a short while as he did so. A troubled look soon came over him, as if something was on the tip of his tongue. Eventually he spoke again. "Your mother told me you were a shy and anxious child. Would you agree with her?"

"Yes, I suppose so."

"Do you have many close friends, Steve?"

"No, not really. I mean there is Marcus, but I've only really known him a few weeks. There are people I went to college with, but no one I would really describe as close. I prefer my own company in all honesty."

"Really? What do you like to do?"

"I like to read, and I like to listen to music."

"Ah yes, you play the guitar I believe?"

"Yeah."

"I dabble a little myself when I can find the time." A silence came over us once again, before Dr. West continued. "Going back to your father and the conversation I had with your mother this morning. She admitted something to me that she was not proud of. Something she has given me permission to discuss with you as part of your therapy. Something that she has never told you before that is going to trouble you greatly." He stopped talking and seemed to study my face, looking for any change in my expression and perhaps pausing to give me the opportunity to speak. But I stayed silent. "You see Steve, although your father did indeed die in a car accident when you were six. The coroner's report concluded that he had died by his own hand. It seems he purposely drove his car into a wall, as an act of suicide. I'm sorry to be the one to tell you this, I can only imagine you were so young when it happened that your mother felt it right to shield you from the truth. She tells me her decision has haunted her ever since."

I sat motionless, staring at the doctor as tears rolled down my cheeks. He plucked a handful of tissues from a box on his desk and walked them around to me. He then poured a small glass of water from a jug that was on a table in the corner of the room and placed this in front of me. "Are you OK, Steve?"

I stammered in my reply. "I just don't know what to make of this?"

"I know this will be incredibly painful to hear, as the truth often is. You mother will have answers for you, I am sure, when you next speak with her. She will be prepared for your questions."

"It was my birthday, my sixth birthday. I was waiting for him to come home from work. I'd been waiting for him all day."

"I'm deeply sorry Steve. I'd like for you to talk about this again. There is strong evidence that certain traits of one's mental health can be hereditary." He walked away with his back to me, studying the many pictures on the wall of his office. "I don't want to fill your head with too much more on our first meeting. I think we've said everything we need to for now." I breathed in sharply and attempted to wipe the tears from my face. "When you go home Steve, I'd like you to attend a weekly appointment with a colleague of mine down in Sussex. Just an hour a week for a couple of months. I really feel some progressive psychiatry would do you the world of good. Really help you open up about your feelings and face up to the past, as it were."

"OK."

"And I'm going to write you a prescription, Citalopram. Something to take the edge off daily life, to help you feel a little less anxious. My colleague, Dr. Roberton, will be able to continue the prescription for as long as he feels is necessary. How does that sound to you?"

"That sounds fine," I replied. "Are you saying I can leave here?"

"Soon Steve. You'll spend tonight with us as we need to monitor you for at least 48 hours under the terms of your stay. We'll meet again tomorrow like I said and have another chat. I feel I can arrange for your mother to come and collect you, if not tomorrow then perhaps the day after. Life is a wonderful gift, and you are a young man with everything to live for. Engage with your therapy and take your medication." He smiled at me. "I understand you were studying English at university, and your mother is hoping you'll return in due course?"

"Hopefully, I'm not too sure."

"Well, I wish you best of luck." He looked at his watch. "Ah, its 5.30 p.m. Time for you to get some dinner. I hope your room will be adequate for tonight, you have a TV and there's a selection of DVDs in the common room for you to choose from. You get yourself a good night's sleep, and I will see you tomorrow."

With that, the doctor clapped his hands together and walked across the room, opening the door and holding it for me.

"Thank you," I said, as I passed him.

Dawn was sat on a chair, when she saw me walk out, she stood up. "Steve, I hope that went well. I'll take you back to your room, and we'll bring you some dinner."

"Thank you. I'm not really feeling very hungry, but I'll try to eat something."

"I'm going to bring a phone to your room also, your friend

51

Marcus has called the hospital asking after you. He's left his number if you'd like to call him back?"

"Maybe tomorrow. I think I'd like to just watch some TV this evening, I'm feeling quite tired."

"Yes, that sounds like a good idea. Come on, lets walk back."

My mind was swimming as she led me back to my room, it felt like it was going to implode with the news I had just been given about my father. I didn't know what this meant, or whether it may have any connection with what was happening to me. I had much to think about.

# Chapter 6.

A couple of hours later, I was laying on my bed having picked at the dinner of sausages, mashed potato, and gravy they had brought me. I was watching TV when Dawn knocked on the door and gave me some medication.

"To help you sleep," she insisted.

It was early evening but there wasn't much reason to spend any more time awake in this place than necessary. My mind was buzzing with everything I had learned throughout my conversations with both Yasmin and Dr. West.

Yasmin had a deeply troubling look across her face while she had studied the palms of my hands. But she had given me a little hope that I could try and understand why this seemingly demonic presence had attached herself to me. There was hope, however small, that I could rid myself of the wretched curse.

The Grey Witch had always appeared when I was at my very lowest, arriving at the precipice of my anguish to call me over to the other side. *But why? Who was I to her? How was I going to look into my past, and what was I going to find while I was there?*

I was also struggling to comprehend what the doctor had told me about my father killing himself. I just couldn't believe that my mother would have kept this from me all these years. True, she had tried her hardest never to speak of him at all, changing the subject as quickly as she could whenever I dared to mention him. However, I was eighteen now. A man. And when I next saw her, she had a lot of explaining to do. I was becoming lost in my thoughts as the medication started to take hold. As the images and sound of the television began to blur, I found myself drifting off to sleep.

* * *

The dreams I had that evening were like nothing I ever had before. I remember the visions vividly as a collage of deeply troubling images flashed through my mind. My father driving in his red Volkswagen Golf with my younger self sitting beside him in the passenger seat. '*Buckle up kid, we're going on one hell of a ride!*'

He had a disturbing look over his face as he hit the acceleration pedal, and I was pinned back in my seat. Drool dribbled from his mouth as he sat hunched forward, peering over the steering wheel and staring wildly into the night, the scar of a childhood accident imprinted on his cheek. He threw the car vicariously around corners and started laughing as he looked at me. '*She's coming for you, little man!*' I tried to scream but, as I did so, I could feel the belt tightening around my neck.

In an instant, I was no longer in the car seat. Instead, I was back in my student accommodation. Only this time, I was hanging from the ceiling gasping for breath, as my legs dangled below me desperately trying to find the floor. I looked down, and Marcus and his oafish friends were all sat around the kitchen table, drinking and laughing. Marcus looked up at me swinging from the rafters. '*Oh, don't mind him lads ... he's already dead!*'

I looked to the window and could see the figure 6 being drawn in the condensation by an invisible finger. My eyes felt like they were bulging from my sockets, until eventually they exploded and everything went dark.

Then I heard my name. "*Stephen ... Steve ... Stevie ...*"

My eyes opened. I was still laying on my hospital bed, dripping with sweat and panting heavily. It was dark. The television was switched off. I looked up and there she was. The Grey Witch was facing me, her back to the ceiling. "*Shhhhhhh.*" she said, her crooked finger raised up across her veil.

In a flash, her body descended from the ceiling towards me, stopping just short of falling onto mine. She hung suspended in the air just a few inches from my face. "*Your time has come,*" she hissed through her veil at me, her long dank hair hanging down and resting on my face. I could feel it, this was real.

I lay there frozen, staring back up at her. With her finger, she slowly removed her veil, and what I saw terrified me. Her lips were a mass of thin parasitic worms, wriggling and writhing around. They began stretching out from her face towards mine, dripping with a foul saliva. She bared her teeth; rancid and green, pointed and sharp. I closed my eyes and heard her laugh, that wretched cackle. And then I felt her move away.

Opening my eyes, I saw her float towards the window. When she reached it, she clicked her fingers on the lock, and I heard it snap open. Then she raised her hands, and the window opened outwards. The Grey Witch turned, her sharp finger once again pointed at me, as she beckoned me over to her.

"*Come!*" she demanded.

I don't know why, I felt as if I was under some kind of trance as I swung my legs across the side of the bed and stood up.

I started walking towards the Witch and the open window beyond her, and she started cackling once again.

"*Juuuump. Take your life and give the soul that was promised to me!*" She moved behind me as I approached the open window. The wind was howling outside as I stood looking out into the night. It was dark and I could not make out any of the garden which sat two stories below.

"*Jump!*"

I was listening to her voice, and I was very close to the edge. I felt a hand on my shoulder, and I shuddered at the thought of her. I looked to where I felt the touch, but instead of the Witch's disgusting talon, there was a small and delicate hand with red nail varnish.

"Stevie, stop!" Standing next to me was Yasmin. The Witch was gone. "She was here, wasn't she?"

I looked into Yasmin's eyes; tears were streaming down my face. I nodded in reply. She put her arm around my shoulder and turned me towards my bed.

"Go and sit down." She looked at the open window. "I'm going to lock this back up. If they find you've opened the window, they'll assume you were planning the worst, and you can kiss goodbye to getting out of here anytime soon." She looked up at the ceiling. "Luckily, they don't have cameras in our private rooms."

I tentatively walked over to the bed, searching the room for any sign of the Grey Witch. I checked under the bed before sitting down. The coast seemed clear.

I watched Yasmin as she pushed the window closed and snapped the padlock into place. "You didn't open that padlock yourself, did you? You couldn't have." She walked across the room to the bed and sat down next to me, putting her hand on my leg to comfort me.

"She was here, Yasmin. She keeps coming for me and I don't know how I can stop her, how I can keep surviving her? She was at my father's funeral, and she tried to drown me in the bath that night."

"How many times have you seen her?"

I was crying so hard I could barely get my words out. "I don't know. I think two more times, maybe three now. She was here and I was going to jump. Oh my god Yasmin, I was going to jump! If you hadn't of been here ..."

Yasmin took each of my hands in hers, turned my palms towards her and studied them. "She comes when you're at your lowest. That's the vessel that allows her to show herself to you. The curse you have is strong, but like all demons she has her limitations. Is this the first time you've seen her since you've been in hospital?"

"I dreamt about her I think."

"I don't think she can harm you in your dreams. Although she may leave her mark there. When you get out of here, I want you to visit someone. My aunt. She lives on the south coast." Yasmin pulled out a small notebook from her pocket and scribbled into it. She then ripped out the page and folded it in half before walking across to where my jeans were laying on a chair and placed the note into a pocket. "My aunt will help you. She taught me how to palm read, but she can see so much more than I can. Visit her, tell her I sent you, and let her give you a reading. She might be able to see who it is that has attached herself to you. She might be able to help you find a way out." Yasmin looked into my eyes, and then she leaned forward and kissed my forehead. "I'd better go back to my room before anyone catches me in here."

She left, closing the door behind her.

\* \* \*

No doubt because of the medication, I found myself falling asleep soon after Yasmin had left my room. The rest of my night was uninterrupted, although my dreams continued to trouble me.

The next morning, I was awakened by an orderly with breakfast in hand. I tried to piece together what was real and what I had dreamed during the night. As I drank a mug of tea, and ate some buttered toast, Dawn knocked on my door and came in. She seemed to be in particularly good spirits.

"Good morning, Steve, I have some great news for you. You must have made a good impression on Dr. West yesterday afternoon. He called your mother after you met with him, and they decided the best place for you to continue your recovery will be at home with her. She's coming to collect you today. You're going home!"

I felt my heart beating fast in my chest at the news. I had convinced myself that I was going to be spending days, if not weeks, in the hospital, and after the night I had just had, I was sure my sanity was going to come into question. I could barely believe what she was telling me, but I needed to remain calm.

"Thank you so much Dawn, I feel like I'm ready to go home. Do you know what time she is coming?" I looked at the clock on the wall, it had just turned 9:30 a.m.

"She's coming at 11 a.m. Dr. West will see you at 10:30 a.m. and sign your release papers, then he'll take you down to meet her in reception." She put her hand on the back of mine. "I wish you the very best, Steve. Get back on your feet and get yourself back to university. I can tell you are going to go far in life." She smiled and winked at me, but as she turned and walked away, I called out.

"Do you think you could please let Yasmin know I'm going home? I'd like to see her to say goodbye. Perhaps in the lounge, if she's free?"

Dawn looked at me, a little puzzled. "Yasmin?"

"Yes. I don't know her surname. She's a patient here, blonde hair, about my age?"

Dawn shook her head. "I'm sorry Steve, I don't know who you mean. You're on a male only ward. You may be thinking of one of the other nurses perhaps, but I don't know anyone with that name." I stared at Dawn, trying to understand the words she had said. "Are you okay, Steve?" she asked.

I didn't hesitate in replying, "Never mind, I'm fine. Just a little sleepy still, I guess. I've not been awake long. Don't worry, and thank you again for all your help these last few days."

Her smile reappeared. "Take care Steve." And with that she left.

I waited for my heart rate to slow and made my way to the shower room. As I washed myself, I ran over what Dawn had just told me. *It couldn't be true. Yasmin must be here.* After I dried myself, I got dressed and remembered the note that Yasmin had placed in my jeans pocket. I reached in and there it was. I plucked it out and unfolded it. The note simply said:

*Griselda – Plum Cottage, Beachy Head Road, Eastbourne.*

I stared at the words, repeating them over in my mind, and I sat down on the bed in a state of panic. The handwriting was unmistakably mine. *This makes no sense.*

I pulled on my jumper and left, heading for the lounge. Inside, there were a dozen or so patients occupying the various chairs, tables and sofas. Dawn was right. They were all male. For the next half an hour or so, I walked around the communal areas of the hospital. I went outside and walked the circumference of the garden. I stopped at the small clearing of trees where I had met Yasmin the previous afternoon. There was no sign of her.

Eventually, I went back to my room to pack. I had come into the hospital with only the clothes on my back, although my mother had dropped off a few essential items which I placed back into the bag she had left.

I made my way to Dr. West's office. It was 10:30 a.m. and I was right on time.

"Come on in," he called, after I had delicately knocked on his door. I entered his office. "Steve, it's good to see you again. I believe your mother is already here and waiting for you downstairs. We think returning home to recover is the best place for you. Just make sure you take it easy, and take your time to get better, before going back to your studies." He handed me a folder. "In here is the medication we discussed which will last you a fortnight. Take a pill now, and again before bed. Repeat each day. I've included the details of your first weekly appointment with my colleague, Dr. Roberton. On your second appointment, he'll renew your prescription. He really will help you get yourself back on track. Now let me take you downstairs. Are you ready to go home?"

I nodded. I was ready to leave, to meet my mother and get some answers. And I was ready to try and put an end to this nightmare once and for all.

\* \* \*

However, as I plummeted from the cliff edge towards the abyss, I realized that even the slightest optimism I might have had when I walked out of Dr. West's office ... was ultimately doomed to fail.

# Part 3 Chapter 1.

Fifteen minutes after Dr. West had taken me down to see my mother, I was seated in the passenger seat of her car. I had barely uttered a word when I first saw her, still angry with her about hiding the truth of my father's death from me. I had also felt more than a little shame as I had been passed into her care by the doctor. When Dr. West had first greeted her, they had stepped to one side and spoken out of my earshot, as if I couldn't be trusted with whatever they were discussing. But ultimately, seeing her again and walking out of the hospital a free man was a relief.

We sat awkwardly together in the car for a while before she finally broke the silence. "I've been so worried about you these last few days Stevie, but I don't want to press you on why you did what you did. When you're ready to talk to me, I'll be here for you. I'll be ready to listen." She paused, waiting for me to reply, but I wanted her to acknowledge first what she knew I'd been told. "Dr. West talked me through the meeting you had yesterday, and I know he told you about your father. I'm so sorry I hadn't spoken to you before and told you the truth. It's just that you were so young when it happened, and you wouldn't have understood. As time went on, it just seemed harder and harder to talk to you about him, and what he did to himself. What he did to us. It was easier for me to try and forget."

"You should have told me, Mum. I had a right to know."

She nodded. "And now you do know. You're a man now, and the time is right. I will try and answer any questions you have as best I can. I am sorry." She touched the back of my hand with hers, then turned the key in the car's ignition, and reversed out of the parking space. We drove out of the car park and onto the streets of London. It would take at least an hour to make it back home to our village in Sussex. I decided it was time to press my mother further.

"Dr. West told me that Dad purposely crashed his car into a wall. That he committed suicide, on my birthday."

"Yes Stevie, that's what the coroner's report told us. Your father was a deeply troubled man, but no one will ever really know what was going through his mind at that moment. They said there was no evidence of the car skidding out of control prior to the crash, that the tire marks showed the car simply turned from the road at speed into a head on impact." She began crying as she spoke. "There were eyewitnesses who came forward and described him as laughing hysterically, with tears running down his cheeks, as he turned the car from the road.

"He had a history of suicide attempts. Overdoses mainly, pills and alcohol. He was an alcoholic. I'm so sorry Stevie, but now it seems to be happening with you, and I don't know what to do." She stopped to catch her breath, trying to control her tears as she drove. "Dr. West has explained to me that this kind of illness can be hereditary. He seems quite convinced your troubles stem from your father, and this is the only sense I can make of what's happening with you."

"I don't want to kill myself, Mum. It's difficult to explain what happened without you thinking I really am crazy. But I think Dad was in some kind of trouble, and I think that trouble has now somehow passed on to me."

"Your father's illness may have been passed to you, but he did not help himself. He was self-medicating with the drink to get through each day, but this could make him violent too. Never with you, he adored you. But with me and others around him. He used to say he was cursed to die young, but his only curse was the bottle he chose."

My ears pricked up as my mother spoke these words. "Curse? What did he say to you about being cursed?"

My mother seemed irritated by this question. "It was just nonsense. He was not a well man."

I unintentionally raised my voice, "Tell me what he said about being cursed!"

"There's nothing to tell, Stevie. He used to speak a lot of nonsense when he was drunk. And if I questioned him or tried to make him see reason he would get angry with me. He would say his family was cursed, his real family. But he was a very complicated man. You know he mainly grew up in the care system, floating around various foster families until he reached eighteen. It doesn't make for the best start in life. He told me that until he was six years old, he lived out of a caravan with his mother and her family, never staying still. They moved over from Ireland when he was just a baby, traveling all over the country from one town to the next. But I'm afraid, other than that, I know very little about your father's life before he met me."

We sat silent for a while, my mind racing with what I was learning about my father.

My mother smiled a little as she continued. "You know he

used to sing old Irish folk songs to you when you were little. Songs he remembered his birth mother used to sing to him. He did have his moments of charm I suppose. I met him when he was just eighteen and you were born within a year. It was all very much a whirlwind really, and we were both very young. Too young for him perhaps."

"Mum," I interrupted. "I need you to tell me what he said about being cursed."

This time, it was my mother who raised her voice, "I told you there was no curse, he was a sick man. I don't want to talk about curses anymore. I shouldn't have mentioned it."

"Yes, you should have, Mum. You should have told me sooner."

She didn't reply. We drove in silence for the next fifteen minutes or so. I just watched the world go by as we moved through the streets of London, and onto the main road that would take us out of the city, and down to the south coast.

"Mum ..."

"Yes darling?"

"What I told you about yesterday, The Witch, it's all true, and I think Dad saw her too. I think she's the reason he died. I think she's the curse he spoke about, and now she's after me." My mother burst into tears again but said nothing in reply. "Please Mum, talk to me."

"I'm crying because you're talking like your father used to. Dr. West thought you were well enough to come home with me, but listening to you now, I'm not so sure. What did he say when you spoke about this witch?"

"I didn't tell Dr. West. I know it sounds crazy, but you've got to believe me, Mum."

She shook her head. "You're sounding like your father and

look where he ended up. Dead. I'm so scared I'm going to lose you too."

I reached over and put my hand on hers which was resting on the gear stick. We didn't speak again for some time, and as we headed down the motorway into Sussex, I dosed off.

\* \* \*

When I awoke, we were driving along the country lanes which would take us into our village. I looked at my mother and smiled. She looked sad and her eyes were puffy from crying.

I looked back out of the front window, and what I saw made me jerk in my seat.

"Mum!" I shouted, as I grabbed the steering wheel, turning it sharply towards me. For standing in the middle of the road, was the Grey Witch. She stared through the windshield, pointing her finger towards me, her shawl blowing behind her in the wind. The car veered sharply to the left and my mother screamed, grabbing the steering wheel with both hands. She pulled the wheel back around to the right as the car left the road and drove up onto a dusty verge. We narrowly avoided crashing into an iron gate before she regained control and we returned to the road. Luckily, there were no other vehicles around us.

I turned back, looking through the rear window, and there she still was. The Witch had turned around to face our car, while my mother brought the vehicle under control and pulled over to the side.

"What the hell did you do that for?" she screamed at me.

"I'm sorry Mum, but keep driving please. Just keep driving!"

"That was a stupid thing to do Stevie, you were sleeping, and you grabbed the wheel from me."

I realized she had not seen The Witch. I didn't want to mention the apparition again, but I knew I needed her to get the car moving.

"I'm sorry, I don't know what happened. Just keep going Mum, please."

I looked behind, and the Grey Witch was moving silently towards our car, only this time she wasn't floating slowly. She was crouched down on all fours, her back arched high in the air with her arms stretched out in front of her, raising her body from the ground with her clawed fingers. She began frantically scuttling towards us.

I started to panic, but fortunately, my mother put her foot on the pedal, and we started to move again. I stared out of the back window and watched as the Witch started to lose ground on us, until eventually she disappeared altogether into the horizon. I realized I was sweating profusely and could not believe what had just happened. The Grey Witch's visits were becoming frequent now.

I realized I was not going to be free of her until I found out who she was and why she wanted me. And it felt like I was running out of time. I thought of the name and address in my jeans pocket and decided I would go see Griselda as soon as possible. Her address was less than ten miles from our village.

A short while later, we pulled into the driveway of the home I had left for university life just a few weeks earlier. It dawned on me that I had merely dipped my toe into trying to live as an independent adult. It had not lasted long, and it had not gone well.

* * *

I went straight to my room after we went inside. I was feeling tired despite it being only lunchtime. I had little appetite to eat anything. My mother agreed that I needed to rest, and as I lay on my bed, I began to formulate a plan to ask whether I could borrow her car to go to the local supermarket. I had passed my test earlier in the summer, and she had always been happy for me to use it. I was hoping that despite everything, she would still let me drive. I reached for my laptop and opened up google, typing in the address from my pocket, *Plum Cottage, Beachy Head Road, Eastbourne.*

The search engine pinpointed the location for me; it was on the coastal cliff road. I could visit Yasmin's aunt, and if she was indeed real and willing to talk to me, I could spend around 30 minutes there before I would need to come back.

Thinking of Yasmin left me feeling confused. I was longing to see and talk to her again. *But had she just been a dream?* If that were the case and she wasn't real, then where the hell did I get Griselda's name and address from? *Was this all a fantasy?*

I walked across my room and looked out of the window, half expecting to see the Grey Witch looking back up at me. But there was no one there. It had started raining and small puddles were beginning to form on the road. I decided to rest for an hour and then go and speak with my mother. I gradually began to fall asleep, and after a while I awoke to a gentle knock on my door. The door opened to reveal my mother standing with a cup in her hand and a shoe box tucked under her other arm. It was my father's box of photos. I hadn't looked through them in years.

"I've brought you some tea," she said, as she walked across the room and placed the cup on my bedside table. "I looked in an hour ago and you were out like a light. You've been asleep for quite some time. How do you feel now?"

"I feel okay, thanks. Better. You've brought Dad's photo box?"

"This?" She placed the shoe box on the bed beside me. "With all this talk of your father, I thought you might like to take a look. I don't think you've looked through it since you were a child." She opened the lid. "Here."

I sat up and investigated the shoe box which was full of photographs. There were pictures of my father with me as a small child, and photos of him with my mother. Photos on the beach, and photos at the zoo. The memories came flooding back to me. But as I flicked through the pictures, one in particular took my eye. I picked it out and looked closer before my heart sank so fast that I felt like throwing up. It was his most cherished photo of all. I turned it over, and sure enough written in pencil on the back was the date – 1973.

I turned it back over, hoping that what I had first seen was an illusion. But it wasn't. This was the photo of my father as a young child with his birth mother. As I looked closely at his mother, the horrifying realization came over me. She was Yasmin. It was unmistakably her, and she looked just as she had in the hospital. Her long blonde hair resting on her shoulders, blue eyes, and a smile that lit up her face.

"You look puzzled, Stevie? That's the photo of your father with his birth mother. It's the only photo he had of her you know. But you've seen it before." She turned it over and looked at the back. "Ah yes, 1973. He was six, the same age as you were when he died. This was taken just before his mother passed away, the year he went into care. He cherished this photo; it was all he had of the childhood he left behind."

I knew for certain ghosts existed now. I knew that curses and phantoms existed, and I felt that I was in so deep with something I would never truly understand. At that moment, I longed for

Yasmin even more ... my grandmother.

"How old was she, when she died?" I asked.

"I'm afraid I don't know, Stevie. But looking at the photo she seems so young. Deep down, I don't think your father ever recovered from losing her and being taken away from his family."

"Do you know a lady called Griselda?"

"No," she replied. "Why do you ask?"

"Oh, it's just a name I remember Dad mentioning when I was little." I lied.

"Well, I don't think he knew anyone by that name. Not that he ever mentioned to me anyway."

I sipped my tea and continued rummaging through the box. There was now a calmness between us, and I decided this would be the right moment to ask her.

"Mum, do you mind if I borrow the car for an hour this afternoon? I'd like to go to the supermarket and get a few things. I can make us some dinner this evening if you like?"

The expression on her face told me she wished I hadn't asked that question.

"I'm not sure you should drive so soon after coming out of hospital, darling. Why don't we go together, and I'll drive?"

"Mum, please. You can trust me. I'm fine. I promise I'll only be gone for an hour. Just to the supermarket and back."

She looked deep into my eyes and forced a smile. "Okay, you can take the car. But please don't be too long. You'll need to put some petrol in though, it's really low after the drive up to London and back this morning." She pulled a £20 note out of her pocket and handed it to me, "Why don't you pick us up a couple of pizzas?"

I took the money from her and gave her a hug. "Thanks Mum,

I will. And thank you for trusting me, it means a lot."

Thirty minutes later, I was pulling out of the driveway as she watched from the door. I had every intention of grabbing us a couple of pizzas. But not before I had paid a visit to my great aunt. I had to know if she was real, and if she was, I hoped she would be able to help me.

# Chapter 2.

As I drove my mother's car, rain poured from the sky. It was around 5 p.m., and the sky had turned dark with clouds as black as death itself. The wind was howling, and it was causing the vehicle to rock slightly as I drove. I made my way out of our village and was soon driving along the country lane that would meander towards the coast up to the Beachy Head cliff road - a road that ran the length of the cliff face for approximately five miles.

There was an old Inn at the top, and just a handful of residential properties dotted along. One being Plum Cottage. I hoped to God that Griselda was real, and that this would indeed be her home. I needed answers, and I needed to know that there was a way to stop this despicable phantom before she took my life.

As I drove up towards the top of the cliff, the weather grew more horrific, and the thought occurred to me that my mother would be worried sick about me driving in this storm. I checked my phone, which only had one bar of signal, there was no contact from her, yet.

I drove for another mile or so before I noticed an opening to a long driveway on my left. I stopped as close as I could to the post box that sat at the entrance. Wiping the condensation from the car window with my sleeve, I could just see the sign which read; *Plum Cottage.*

I turned into the driveway, following along towards the cottage while the wind and rain howled against my mother's car. The windscreen wipers worked furiously on the highest setting. The driveway to Plum Cottage was like a dirt track, I could sense the mud spraying up the sides of the car and it dawned on me I would have to find a car wash on my way back home. It had gotten really dark now and my visibility was poor, but the driveway soon opened out into a small turning area in front of the cottage. I stopped the car and turned off the ignition.

Pulling the hood of my jumper over my head as I exited the vehicle, I quickly slammed the car door shut behind me and ran up to the front of the building. Luckily, there was an open porch area, so when I reached the large oak front door I was mostly sheltered from the rain.

The cottage looked as if it was hundreds of years old, and even in the pouring rain, the musky smell of the old building hung pungent in the air. There was no bell, just a large cast iron knocker with the carving of an angel holding the heavy looking ring. I knocked loudly three times and waited. There was no sound from within the cottage that I could hear over the rain, and no-one answered the door. I knocked another three times, and this time, I could hear shuffling from the other side, and the sound of jangling metal before a key was turned in the lock.

The door opened part way, and an elderly lady peered out at me through the crack. She looked to be around seventy years old, with dark graying hair hanging limply down to her shoulders. Small glasses were perched on the end of her nose.

"Yes?" She asked.

"I'm sorry to disturb you madam. I'm looking for a lady called

73

Griselda. I believe she lives here at Plum Cottage?"

She straightened her glasses and peered at me. "Oh, you are, are you?" she asked, with a thick Irish accent. "And who might you be?"

"My name's Stephen McCarthy. My father's mother was named Yasmin. I think she was your niece."

The elderly lady took in a sharp breath and slowly nodded her head. "I am Griselda. How did you find me?"

My heart skipped a beat as I realized she was indeed real, and now standing before me. I drew a deep breath and answered.

"Yasmin gave me your address, she said you would be able to help me."

Griselda snorted in disgust. "I doubt that very much young man, my niece has been dead for the last thirty years. Try again."

"I'm not lying to you, I promise. I've seen her. Just yesterday, I saw her clear as day and she looked, well, she looked like she was barely a few years older than me."

She took off her glasses and wiped her eyes with a crumpled handkerchief produced from her pocket. "Well, in that case Stephen McCarthy, I guess you had better come in." She pulled the chain off the lock and fully opened the door, walking away as she did so. "Please close the door behind you and follow me."

I did as I was told and walked through a dusty hallway into her living room. It was small and cramped. An antique looking wooden table with two chairs sat in the corner next to a window, while opposite, sat a two-seater sofa and an armchair. The furniture was patterned with flowers and looked nearly as old as Griselda herself. There was a large Inglenook fireplace ablaze with flames in the center of the main wall. And there was a shelf, bursting with leather bound books. She had no television set.

Griselda sat in the armchair and pointed towards the sofa. "Sit down, please." Again, I did as I was told. "Now Stephen, you're telling me you've seen my niece, Yasmin. My niece who died long before you were born. And as far as I know, the little boy who became your father is also dead. Are you going to tell me you've seen him too?"

"No ma'am, I haven't."

"Have you seen any other ghosts, Stephen?"

"I have. I've seen a Witch. At least I think that's what she is."

Griselda looked saddened as the words left my lips. "Dear God," she said, looking up to her ceiling and making the sign of the cross on her chest.

"Yasmin said you could read my palm, and that you might be able to tell me who the Witch is. She keeps coming for me, and I don't think she's going to stop until I'm dead. Please help me, I'm so scared."

Griselda took my hands in hers and gazed across my palms, holding them tight and gently shaking them as she did so. She looked up into my eyes. "What do you know about your father's childhood, Stephen? What do you know about his mother?"

"Very little," I replied, producing from my pocket the photo from 1973. "I'd seen this photo when I was young, my dad would show it to me. But I met Yasmin while I was in hospital these last few days. And then today, I realized she was the lady in this photo. She was his mother."

Griselda reached out and took the photo from me, smiling as she did so. "Do you want to know something?" she asked. "I took this. It was the last photo of your father and his mother before she died, and before he was taken from us. I'm going to tell you what happened, Stephen. I'm going to tell you why this apparition has been haunting you. But first, I need you to think very carefully and answer one question for me. How many times

75

have you seen this Witch?"

I recounted the experiences I had had with her in my head. "I've seen her five times," I replied.

"And each time, have you come close to death, Stephen?"

"Very close." I nodded.

"Well, you're a remarkable young man, and very lucky to be alive then. I believe she will come for you once more, but once more only. If you can survive her one last time, you'll never see her again. Here, look ..."

She put the tip of her finger into my palm and traced one continuous line on my hand, making the figure six. I was surprised that I had never noticed this before, but there it was clear as day. It then occurred to me at that very moment, that the scar I remembered from my father's cheek also resembled the same number. I also recalled the Witch writing the number six in the condensation of my window.

"You've been marked by an immensely powerful curse, Stephen. One that I'm afraid has been passed down to you from your father, a curse from the depths of Hell itself. Do you know that the number six is representative of the devil? It is a powerful number, one that can align dimensions if one knows how. I'm going to try and explain this to you as best I can." She paused and picked up an old wooden pipe that lay next to a book on a small table by her chair. She lit a match and took a long draw on the pipe, blowing the smoke out towards the crackling fireplace.

# Chapter 3.

"When your father was born, Yasmin lived with me and her mother, my twin sister Esmé. Yasmin's father had died when she was just a baby girl, stabbed in a bar fight back in the old country. Yasmin would never tell us who the father of her baby was. She knew he wouldn't be safe if her mother found him. Yasmin was only fifteen when she fell pregnant, you see. We lived what we called a free lifestyle back in those days, traveling around the country living in our converted bus. The summer Yasmin fell pregnant, we'd traveled from fair to fair, from week to week, as we had always done. There were dozens of them the length and breadth of the country. Your grandfather probably never even knew he'd had a child." She smiled to herself, seemingly lost in her memories.

"We were a family of palm and tarot card readers, mystics if you like. And that is how we made our money. If we had been born hundreds of years before, the three of us might have been looked upon very differently. They would have called us a *Coven*, if you understand my meaning?"

I nodded, listening intently to every word she spoke.

"*Cailleach* we would have been called. The three of us were very much like our ancestors, the power of clairvoyance had always been strong for the women in our family. Yasmin's mother, your great grandmother I suppose, was far more powerful with the gift than either me or her daughter was. Her sight was something quite miraculous. But the older she got, the more reclusive Esmé became. Distancing herself from both me and her daughter.

"She would study her books day and night, obsessively reading everything she could about the occult. Honing her own magic in a way that quite honestly frightened both Yasmin and me. She became obsessed with the darker side of our history, and that was very dangerous when mixed with the power she had inherited through our bloodline."

"Is Esmé still alive?" I asked.

Griselda shook her head. "No Stephen, she is not." As she continued speaking, the hairs on my arms were tingling. Her words sent shivers down my spine. "Everything changed for us when Yasmin fell pregnant and had your father. Unbeknownst to her, Esmé was initially considering performing an abortion. But I did everything I could to stop her, to convince her not to. Yasmin grew scared of her mother, but she knew I would always do what I could to protect her. When your father, little Michael was born, I delivered him myself in a field under the moonlight; as generations in our family had always been born before him. We were shocked at first to discover he was a boy. Esmé had reluctantly made her peace with the fact that our number would be growing by one, but in our family, we only ever gave birth to girls. And Esmé scolded me that night for convincing her to let her daughter have the child. She saw little Michael as some kind of bad omen."

Griselda was no longer smiling at the memories that seemed

to be coming to her in waves.

"We continued our life once Michael came along. Yasmin bonded with him at once, and he was like my own grandchild. And Esmé, well she accepted the baby, I suppose, in her own way. But she was always extremely strict with him and his mother.

"We had to be careful regarding the local authorities as we traveled around, making sure we skipped from county to county quickly. Never stopping in any one place for too long. Questions get asked, you see, when anyone takes too much notice of a small child in our community. As the years went on, and your father became a toddler, I very much took on the role of home schooling him and did what I could to keep everyone happy.

"But Yasmin was growing weary with the life we were providing him, and she confided in me that she wanted to settle down in one place. She wanted him to go to a state school and live with stability among children his own age. She had a dream of her and little Michael living together in a house overlooking the sea. She wanted to speak with the social services to see if she could be provided with accommodation. But she kept this from her mother who would have forbid it."

Griselda paused to wipe a tear from her eye with the corner of her sleeve. "Esmé and I grew up traveling and she insisted on no other lifestyle for her daughter. By this time, she was so distant from us both, preferring to spend most of her time alone reading her books. I was fearful of the arts I could see she was dabbling in. As I would listen to her chanting in our ancient language at night, I became terrified that she would use the magic she was exploring to one day inflict harm or punishment on someone. The more Esmé withdrew from us, the more I feared for the future of your father.

"I eventually agreed with Yasmin that I thought her idea

to speak with the authorities was a good one, but that she must absolutely do so without Esmé's knowledge. And that her mother must never know where she settles down.

"We were camped and staying in a field on the edge of Epping Forest when Yasmin had traveled into the nearest town with Michael to present herself to the social services department at the town hall. But it turned out that speaking with them was the worst possible idea she could have had, and her meeting did not go as she would have hoped. When they discovered your father had been born outside of a hospital and was living a transient lifestyle with no permanent address, they expressed their concern. And that evening they sent two social workers down to meet us where we were staying.

"Esmé, of course, discovered what her daughter had been up to behind her back, what I had been complicit in. She was terribly angry with us both. Yasmin was served a paper telling her that she had 24 hours to willingly hand your father over to the authorities, so that he could be taken into temporary care while they tried to formulate a long-term plan with us moving forwards. He was only six bless him. The alternative was that he would be taken into care anyway, by force if necessary. And he would be put up for adoption with Yasmin never having the legal right to know where he was placed. The social worker had a court order, and they advised they would return the following day, leaving us with a warning that officers would be watching our camp site in the meantime. We were given strict instructions not to leave the area.

"And that night, Esmé was furious with her daughter. An enormous row broke out between us all, I'd never seen so much anger from my sister before. She struck Yasmin in front of me, cutting her lip and bloodying her nose. Your father who was just the sweetest little boy was utterly terrified. Yasmin was distraught and she left your father with me, saying she was going to go for a walk in the woods to try and clear her head.

"When she didn't return after an hour, I left Michael with Esmé and went to look for her. After around fifteen minutes of searching the woods, I found her. She was hanging by her neck from the branch of a tree, her legs swaying in the wind.

"It was the single worst moment of my life. Yasmin was clearly already dead as I climbed up and cut the rope she had used, both of us sent tumbling down to the ground under the weight of her lifeless body. I lay there sobbing, holding my niece who I had loved like a daughter since the day she was born. When I eventually looked up, Esmé was standing there watching us, your innocent little father holding her hand.

"*Help us!* I shouted. But she just stood there staring. A black candle burning in one hand, your father's palm in her other. The next thing I knew, the woodland was illuminated by flashlights. It turns out the social worker and her colleague had indeed been watching us, and had followed Esmé and your father down into the woods with a couple of police officers. One ran over to where me and Yasmin were laying, shouting for us not to move as he did so, while the other was frantically calling into his radio for an ambulance to be deployed. Yasmin was pulled from me, and the officer started giving her mouth-to-mouth resuscitation. But it was too late.

"The whole time this was going on, Esmé just stood there. But then she started chanting in our old Gaelic mother tongue. The social worker approached her demanding that she hand-over your father, but Esmé held on to him tight and continued chanting. Her eyes had rolled into the back of her head as she turned to the social worker and hissed. The social worker grabbed your father's arm, he was crying, screaming for his *Mumma.*

"Esmé bent down and started scratching his face with her fingernail, cutting him so he was bloody. She kept repeating the number *six* in some part of a Satanic verse as she did so. I knew that she was trying to conjure an evil spirit. As she attacked your father, the social worker pulled him towards her. The officer, who had called for the ambulance, stood behind Esmé. He began edging closer and closer towards her. He suddenly lunged forward and hit her over the head with his baton. Esmé sunk to the ground, I can remember her body twitching as she did so. And she lay there, blood pouring from her head."

\* \* \*

Griselda paused, a look of horror on her face. I was hanging on every word that she was saying, trying to understand what she was telling me about my father and his mother. It was so sad to imagine him as a child, witnessing the death of his mum while being attacked by the grandmother who never loved him.

She filled her pipe back up with a dark tobacco and took another smoke. "My world ended that night. I lost Yasmin, my niece who had become my best friend in the world. And I lost little Michael who I had helped raise, as he was whisked away by the authorities and taken from me. I had also lost my sister to something far darker.

"Esmé spent a week in a coma before she finally passed away of her head injury. And the strangest thing happened in the hospital one evening as I sat with my sister, not knowing where else to go or what else to do. She opened her eyes for a brief moment and looked into mine. Esmé whispered to me – *Mallacht*

– and I knew your father was damned, cursed to live a miserable life away from his family. The police officer that hit her was suspended, but he kept his job after a full investigation. His defense was that he acted to save your father, and in a way, he was right of course.

"I attended a burial for both Yasmin and Esmé. I was the only one there, we had no one else. I had them buried next to each other in a cemetery close to the forest where they had both died.

"A couple of days after that fateful night, I was visited by one of the social workers. She explained that Michael was going to be kept in care and would be adopted by a family who would look after him better than I ever could. As his paternal Aunt, I would have the right to apply through the courts for accompanied visits with my nephew, however they knew I never would. I didn't have the necessary identification or paperwork to do so. The social worker asked if your father had any belongings they could collect. I put together a bag with a few of his favourite cuddly toys, as well as this photo of him and his *Mumma,* as he called Yasmin – the photo you've brought back to me today." Griselda paused, she had tears in her eyes as she sat back in her chair and lit her pipe once more.

"The words that Esmé spoke when she cut my father's face. What did they mean?" I asked.

"Yes, my dear. This is what you've come to me for today isn't it? One thing's for sure; I was the only person in the woods that night who could ever understand what she was saying. I've lived with those words ever since and researched their meaning with every single book I could find. At the time, I couldn't know for sure whether Esmé had any true power."

"What did she do, what did she say?"

"I believe she conjured a powerful and malevolent entity that

83

evening. *An ancient Witch who imprinted herself on the soul of your father. Caol, the mother of Demons. A legend in our history with the power to take a life. An eye for an eye. Esmé cursed your father for being born and tearing apart her family, for causing Yasmin to take her own life. She whispered that if your father should ever have a son, he must take his own life before his son turns six. Otherwise, the curse would pass onto the child, granting Caol six chances to take the life of that boy herself. I have read such darkness about this Witch. Caol is a collector of souls, and a manifestation of despair, who compels her victims to take their own lives, damning their afterlife to her. I believe that many people labeled psychotic, or schizophrenic, have been victims of Caol over the centuries.*"

I ran the words Griselda had spoken over in my mind. And then it dawned on me. "My father did take his own life, but not before I turned six. He died on my birthday. She first came for me the night of his funeral."

"The curse my sister used is an old one. I inherited many of our culture's ancient texts after she died, but I never wanted to delve into the dark side of the arts like she did. We had made our money telling fortunes, but I preferred to pass on good news. To see the joy in someone's face who didn't quite know whether to believe what I was telling them was true or not. I gave hope to many. But after I lost my sister, my niece, and her child, I sold our bus. And with the money I made and my life savings, I was able to buy this cottage. I wanted to live close to the sea, just as Yasmin had dreamed she would do, and I've stayed here ever since.

"The social worker informed me that Michael had been placed with a family in Eastbourne here on the coast, but I was never allowed to know his address. I felt that by living close by, I may be able to project a positive energy over him. Sounds foolish, I know." She paused a while. "But my heart sank when I read his name in the obituaries in the local paper all those years ago." Tears ran down her cheek as she said this. Griselda wiped her face with her sleeve again, and then leaned forward and took my hand. "You say that Yasmin sent you here to see me, did she give you this address?"

"She did, although I know that sounds crazy."

Griselda smiled. "I've seen her too, talked to her on many occasions. But only ever in my dreams. Now, I know she's always been here with me."

And following those words, for the first time since I had arrived at Plum Cottage, we both sat in a mutual silence.

# Chapter 4.

I was listening to the rain pouring down the window, whilst the fire crackled in the hearth. I wasn't sure what to say next. Her story had both moved and terrified me at the same time. A dip of my toe into the ocean of my father's past that I would surely never forget. I finally had the answer as to why I was being haunted. And from what she had said, it seemed that if I was visited again and somehow survived one more attempt on my life by this demon, then perhaps I would be free.

But I feared beyond comprehension seeing the Grey Witch again, and I did not know how I might survive her if I did. Being alive, in that moment, seemed more like sheer luck to me than anything else. I stared into the fireplace, my thoughts racing while the wind howled outside, and the rain hit her window so hard I thought it may break. I looked at my phone which I saw now had no signal at all and checked the time. I realized I had been listening to her talk for nearly an hour.

"Shit, I've got to get going. I've borrowed my mother's car and well, let's just say she's going to be very worried about me if I don't get back soon."

"That's okay, Stephen. I truly wish I could help you more, but other than telling you what I have, I'm afraid there's little more I can do."

"No, thank you, you've told me everything I needed to know."

I stood up and hurried towards the door, feeling panicked as I did so. I thanked Griselda once again for her time, as she caught up to me and opened the front door. I then ran from her porch to try and stop myself from getting drenched from the rain.

The wind was so strong that I initially struggled to open the car door, and when I eventually sat inside, I could barely see Griselda as she watched me from her doorstep. I started the engine, which spluttered into life due to the rain having soaked the vehicle. Then I turned the car around, and made my way down her driveway.

As I pulled back out onto the Beachy Head Road, the vehicle's dashboard beeped, and the petrol tank symbol started glowing red. I remembered the car had almost been out of fuel when I left home. I checked my phone, still no signal.

As I drove along the cliff road, my mind was already racing with what I had learned about my family's history. But now, I was starting to seriously panic about my current predicament. If I ran out of fuel up here, my only choice would be to run back to Griselda's for shelter and ask to use her phone, if she had one. I hadn't seen one while I was there. She certainly didn't have a television, and what use would she have of a phone, with no one to call? She'd lived the last thirty years as a recluse.

If I got stranded up here and had no way of contacting my mother, she would go out of her mind with worry. I saw a lay-by ahead of me and decided to pull over. The windscreen wipers were barely providing me with a clear view ahead, and I needed to try and clear my head so I could think. I also needed to try and find some phone signal so I could at least text my mum and let her know I was OK. I pulled the car over and turned off the engine. My heart was palpitating. I closed my eyes and took in three deep breaths to try and clear the anxiety from my mind.

As I drew my third breath, I heard even louder breathing in my ear, and I felt a sharp pressure on the back of my neck. My eyes burst open. I looked in the rear view mirror and there behind me, leaning forward from the back seat of the car, was the being I now knew was named *Caol*. She had returned. Her razor tipped fingers were coiling around my neck, her nails scratching and stabbing at my skin. I screamed for my life and closed my eyes, and the intense pain I had felt around my neck disappeared.

My eyes opened and I looked into the mirror. She was gone. I turned the key in the ignition and could only listen as the car failed to turn over. I turned the key again, and nothing. The car would not start. The engine may have flooded; the fuel may have run out. I was scared, and now I was isolated, I felt trapped and claustrophobic.

"*Stephen McCarthy ...*" came a voice from beside me. I turned towards the passenger seat and looked straight into the yellow eyes of *Caol*.

As I gasped, her hands shot forward and grabbed my wrists. Her fingers were coiling around my arms, holding me tight. Her veil dropped to reveal her vile mouth, pulsating, as the parasitic looking worms writhed from her lips, reaching towards me as they had done in the hospital. When she opened her mouth to speak, maggots dropped from the corners onto her lap, and onto the floor of the car.

"*Your soul belongs to Caol, promised to me by Esmé McCarthy thirty years ago. I have been waiting patiently for you, Stephen. Kill yourself and finally give yourself to me!*"

As she spat out these last words with her venomous tongue,

her yellow eyes popped from their sockets and lay dangling on her cheeks. Her grip tightened on my wrists and her body started convulsing. She began cackling, a sound I had now become accustomed to.

I screamed, shaking and pulling my arms from her grip as hard as I could. I shook them free. Turning away from her, I fumbled, but managed to open the car door, kicking it against the wind. I escaped the vehicle and started running from the car as fast as I could. Looking back over my shoulder, I could see the demon was also slipping out of the driver's side of the vehicle. Her body extended, her veil was once more covering her face.

She began moving towards me, gaining speed, with her arms reaching like tentacles, leading her towards me. *How am I going to survive her this final time?*

There was no one around to save me. *Where could I possibly run to?* I looked forward, trying to make my legs move faster, until my senses suddenly forced me to stop. And I did so only just in time, as I had come to the precipice of the cliff edge.

I peered over, a drop of 500ft down onto crashing waves was all that awaited me. I stood in contemplation. Jumping, and committing suicide seemed my only option.

Damned be what would happen to me in the afterlife. In this moment I did not care, and I gave in to defeat. The Witch stood watching me, she was calling me to the sea, willing me to jump and end the terror. And in that moment, I had no fight left in me.

She had won, and I jumped.

# Chapter 5.

T he last vision I saw before I closed my eyes and leapt, was that of my tormentor. I felt as if I was under some kind of hypnosis that was calling me to my fate. A fate bestowed on me by a demented great-grandmother who had seemingly lost her grip on reality. The power that *Caol* held over me was all encompassing.

As I fell, the key moments of her impact on my life had indeed flashed before my eyes, how slowly or quickly they had come to me I did not know. I felt as if I was in some kind of oblivion, suspended in a purgatory of my own making.

My subconscious had initially been awaiting the impact of either the rocks, or the powerful waves below. But it was as if I was dreaming, the visions of my past playing clearly in my mind, and I was hung, in another realm of sorts. I saw only darkness, and I had not yet felt the pain of my fall coming to its catastrophic conclusion.

A light illuminated before me. Distant at first, a pinprick at the end of a long tunnel. *Is this as they said it would be?* If I follow the light, will I find my way to an afterlife? And just what, or who, would be waiting for me when I got there? Will I awake in some kind of paradise, or will my soul forever be damned now that it belonged to *Caol?*

The light was drawing closer, and with it came a sound that started to over-power my senses; a tremendous mechanical whirring noise that grew louder as the light drew closer. I opened my eyes, the bright light shining directly into them, and I heard a voice break through the industrial noise.

"He's alive! He's opened his eyes!"

The voice then called to me directly, "Please stay as still as possible and try to remain calm. This is the coastguard, and we are going to rescue you. Everything is going to be OK."

All of a sudden, the reality of the situation began to dawn on me. I was hanging, suspended in the air. Trapped and covered in the thorns of a gigantic wild bush that was attached to the side of the cliff face.

I looked down and fear hit me like a sledgehammer. Below me, sat the jagged rocks at the foot of the cliff, with wave after violent wave of the roaring sea attacking the shoreline. My legs were dangling below me, I guessed I must have been suspended 100 feet in the air. I realized in that moment that the thorny branches of this giant bush had broken my fall and held onto my body. I frantically looked around, and it became clear that the noise I was hearing was that of a helicopter, which sat floating in the sky a short distance above me. My arms were scratched and bleeding profusely, there was blood running down my face.

A figure in a crash helmet was being lowered down from the helicopter, and when he stopped next to me, he reached across and tied a rope tight around my waist, attaching our bodies together with a metal clip. He started shouting, trying to make himself heard against the noise of the rotating helicopter blades, as well as the howling of the wind and rain.

"It's okay buddy, I've got you. You're one lucky son of a bitch!

Not many people jump from here and live to tell the tale. This is going to hurt a little, you're tangled up rather good. But I've got to get you up to the chopper as quickly as I can."

Beachy Head is a known spot for suicides, one of the highest rates in the world. And when a car is discovered parked in a lay-by just meters from the cliff edge, and the driver's side door left hanging open with no-one around, the worst is assumed. The emergency services would have been called, and the coastguard deployed to search for a body on the rocks at the bottom of the cliff.

The helicopter crew must have been surprised when their search lights instead came across my body hanging from the cliffs. And they must have been even more surprised to have found me alive. But alive they found me, and I thank God they did.

My waist was attached to my rescuer, and he began to try and clear the brambles and branches away from my face as best he could. Then he looked up and made a signal with his hand. Suddenly, a strong hoist began to pull our bodies upward. The thistles and brambles pulled and tore at my flesh as I was yanked free, and what followed is a blur.

We must have safely made it onto the helicopter, as the next thing I remember is laying on my back. People fussing around me, ripping open my shirt and attaching tubes to my arms and pads to my chest. My whole body was in excruciating pain. I was conscious but I had little feeling in my legs. And then as a resuscitation mask was placed over my face and began pumping oxygen into my lungs, I fainted.

# Chapter 6.

So, this is my confession. A therapeutic aid into my mental and physical recovery whilst I try to make sense of the affliction I had been cursed with before I was even born. I spent many weeks in hospital following my fall from grace on that stormy Autumn night. My body was broken in all sorts of different places, while skin grafts were required to heal the injuries I had suffered when the gigantic wild thorn bush, growing out of the side of the cliff face, had broken my fall and saved my life.

I had likely hung there for some time, as I dreamed my life story and the encounters with the demonic Witch who had tried to claim my soul. She had surely thought she had won and I was hers, but she was once again wrong. I had survived.

Of course, my medical records now show that the day I was released from hospital, following a suicide attempt by hanging, I seemingly traveled to the cliffs to throw myself to my death - only to be rescued and brought straight back into hospital once again. But this time, my broken body needed extensive healing before the doctors got to work on my troubled mind.

My mother was naturally distraught. In the early days of my recovery, where I was barely conscious for more than a few minutes at a time, I can remember her sitting by my hospital bed. Sobbing. Crying for her son.

As I began to heal, and was able to talk with her, she promised me that she would do everything she could to make me better. I decided not to tell her about my trip to see Griselda, or my final encounter with the Grey Witch, the demon *Caol*.

It was all over. I would never see the witch again. I had survived six attempts on my life, and according to Griselda, I would now be free of the curse. *The Curse of Six*.

My father was six-years old when he was taken away from his family, in the hours following the tragedy of his mother's suicide. I was six years old when the demon first came for me. She'd had six chances to claim my soul. *Six, Six, Six ...* the number of the beast, indeed.

I spent the following few months in hospital and again played ball with the doctors. No mention of witches or curses. I embraced the therapy I was provided with and took my time to convince everyone that I had spent long enough under their care, that I could be released to get on with my life. I promised I would no longer be any threat to myself.

At first, I expected to see Yasmin; to discover she was yet again in there with me. But I never did. As time went on, the expectation soon disappeared.

One morning, I wrote a letter to Griselda at Plum Cottage. It simply said; *I survived - Thank You. I will come and see you again one day. Love Steve.*

It dawned on me, when I sent the note, that in my rush to leave Griselda's cottage I had left her with the photo of Yasmin and my father. A photo that I could see had meant so much to her when she saw it for the first time in three decades, and this made me smile.

94

* * *

I had handwritten my story in a notebook during my hospital stay, wondering whether one day it might make for a good tale that others may wish to read. Reading was such a huge part of my life you see, and making my way through a number of books brought to me by my mother, really had been instrumental in helping me get through my long hospital stay.

At the beginning of February in 2004, I returned home to my mother, a new man. Upon leaving the hospital, I actually felt free for the first time. Free of the hospital, free of the curse. And I felt that I had my whole life ahead of me. A life worth living.

That summer, my mother and I celebrated my nineteenth birthday, and it was around this time that I also finally decided not to return to university. I wanted to remain close to her, for the time being anyway.

I took a job in a local independent bookstore in the town next to our village, just a short bus ride each day. And I was happy. I had not seen *Caol* again, nor did I think I ever would. Occasionally a shadow in the corner of my eye would make me jump. But whenever I would turn to look, it was always just that ... a shadow, nothing more.

One afternoon I was working alone behind the counter of the bookstore, tapping away on the computer screen and completing the final orders for our online customers that day, a book sitting open on the desk next to me. I heard the ringing of a bell, the tell-tale sign that a customer had just opened the door to our shop and would be coming in to peruse our extensive shelves. I heard footsteps as they made their way left towards the Horror and Sci-Fi section. *My kind of person,* I thought to myself. I looked up and saw a beautiful young woman with flowing blonde hair, wearing a summer dress and large Ray-Ban sunglasses.

She turned to me, and caught me by surprise when she said, "Steve, is that you?"

I immediately thought of Yasmin and felt a panic in my heart. If she had returned to me, what would this mean? Was it possible that the curse had not ended after all?

She walked toward me, lifting the sunglasses from her face, and I felt relief as I realized it was not Yasmin. It was Polly. A face I had not seen for nearly three years.

"Steve, it is you!" She smiled and approached the front of my counter. My panic had turned to anxiety, but I'll admit her smile had made me feel a little more comfortable, and I knew I had to try and play it cool.

"Hi Polly. It's great to see you, it's been a long time."

"That it has," she smiled. "I've just come back after my first year at uni. I'm studying English up in Edinburgh, it's been lovely to be back home up there. How are you?" The smile left her face. "My mum told me that you've been going through quite a tough time?"

People talked in a small community and what she said had not surprised me. "Yeah, it's been a difficult year to say the least. But hey, I'm all good now. I've got this job, and I'm feeling really well. Everything's much better now, thank you."

Her smile returned. "I want to apologize as well, for how things ended between us. It's something that often plays on my mind. I know I should have spoken to you at the time. I should have never treated you that way, I'm sorry."

This apology surprised me. "That?" I replied. "That was nothing, it was so long ago, and we were just kids. Anyhow, you've got nothing to feel sorry for, it was all my fault. And it's all in the past."

Polly nodded her head in agreement, then laughed. "I came in here to pick up the new Stephen King." She acknowledged the open book on my counter. "I can see you're already reading it. That doesn't surprise me."

"Yeah, it's really good. Here let me get you one." I walked over to the window display I had put together and picked up a copy. I returned and rang it through the counter. Polly paid with her card, and I popped the book into a small carrier bag for her. "Well," I said, "It's been really nice to see you."

"It has been nice. I'll look forward to reading this." She turned and walked toward the exit. As she approached the door, she turned back to me. "You must be closing up soon. Do you fancy grabbing a coffee?"

This, I was certainly not expecting. "That would be great," I replied. "I can meet you over the road at Starbucks in around fifteen minutes, if that's okay?"

"Perfect, I'll see you there. I'll make a start on this in the meantime," she said as she held up the carrier bag with her book inside.

"Polly ..."

"Yes Steve?"

"Thank you for coming in to see me."

"You're welcome. I'll see you again shortly."

With that, she walked out of the store with the door clipping shut behind her, the bell left ringing in my ear ... the only sound in an otherwise silent room.

And in that moment, I felt truly at peace.

*** END ***

## About the Author

From a young age, Mark immersed himself within the world of genre storytelling. Devouring paperbacks from the likes of Stephen King & Clive Barker, while immersing himself in the movies of John Carpenter & David Cronenberg. All combining to lay the foundations for a life-long love of Horror, Fantasy & Sci-Fi, which has naturally transcended into a passion for telling his own tales.

A number of his short stories can be found online in places such as Crystal Lake Publishing's Patreon, and The Dark Corner blog. Mark is publishing his own on-going flash-fiction series 'The Curious Dark' on www.kult-zilla.com – where he also writes plenty of Horror adjacent non-fiction.

'The Curse of Six' is his debut novella with RDG BOOKS PRESS, while 'A Slow Decay of Flowers' follows in 2026 via Baynam Books Press.

Mark can be found online in all the usual places!

**You can connect with me on:**

🌐 http://www.kult-zilla.com

🐦 https://x.com/MarkTBates

# Also by Mark T. Bates

'The Curious Dark' on www.kult-zilla.com – where he also writes plenty of Horror adjacent non-fiction.

'A Slow Decay of Flowers' follows in 2026 via Baynam Books Press.

Also Available from RDG BOOKS PRESS
'It's Dark in Their Minds - Horror Anthology Vol I'
'There Will Never Be A Rainbow'
'The HERO The FEAR and The DATE'

Printed in Dunstable, United Kingdom